"Why didn't the intruder take anything?" Erin asked.

Jack voiced his thought. "If nothing was taken, maybe someone has a more personal reason to break in."

In this isolated setting, a half-mile from the edge of a small, resort-area village, with a dense, dark pine forest and a lake beyond the trees, anyone could find easy cover out here.

"I haven't lived up here since I graduated from high school. I can't imagine who it could be," she said.

She managed to present a casual air, yet he'd seen a flare of fear in her eyes, and the way she jammed her trembling hands into the pockets of her apron. She was sure there had been someone here...and she had an idea of who it could be.

But was it someone from her own past...or his?

Books by Roxanne Rustand

Love Inspired Suspense

*Hard Evidence
*Vendetta
*Wildfire
Deadly Competition
**Final Exposure

*Snow Canyon Ranch
**Big Sky Secrets

ROXANNE RUSTAND

lives in the country with her family and a menagerie of pets that frequently find their way into her books. If not working at her day job as a registered dietitian, writing at home in her jammies, or spending time with her family, you'll find her riding one of the family's horses, playing with her camera or hiding with her nose in a book.

She is the author of twenty-three romantic suspense and heartwarming relationship novels. Her first manuscript won the Romance Writers of America Golden Heart Award, and her second was a Golden Heart Award finalist. She was a *Romantic Times BOOKreviews* Career Achievement Award nominee in 2005, and won the magazine's award for Best Superromance of 2006.

She loves to hear from readers, and can be reached by snail mail at Box 2550, Cedar Rapids, Iowa 52406-2550 or through www.roxannerustand.com.

FINAL EXPOSURE
ROXANNE RUSTAND

Steeple
Hill®

Published by Steeple Hill Books™

STEEPLE HILL BOOKS

Steeple
Hill®

ISBN-13: 978-0-373-44353-6

FINAL EXPOSURE

Copyright © 2009 by Roxanne Rustand

www.SteepleHill.com

Printed in U.S.A.

Send forth your light and your truth, let them guide me; let me bring peace to your holy mountain, to the place where you dwell.

—*Psalms* 43:3

Don't worry about anything; instead, pray about everything. Tell God what you need, and thank him for all he has done. If you do this, you will experience God's peace, which is far more wonderful than the human mind can understand. His peace will guard your hearts and minds as you live in Jesus Christ.

—*Philippians* 4:6-7

For Larry, with love and thanks for all that you've been to me. You are my true hero.

ONE

Erin Cole shivered away an uneasy feeling as she unlocked the door of Millie's Provisions and stepped into her new life. The cold. Surely it was only the cold that raised goose bumps on her arms and sent an eerie premonition racing through her mind.

A silly, city-girl reaction to the loneliness of the mountains after being away for so long.

Nothing ever happened in Lost Falls, so there was no reason to be afraid. The peaceful little village, with its few dozen touristy businesses trailing along the shore of Bear Island Lake, swelled with vacationers and bumper-to-propeller traffic during the summer, then slept quietly with only a handful of year-round residents to brave the long winters.

She'd come back to put old ghosts to rest once and for all. She was past all that, and didn't plan to give in to the old fears that had dogged her for so many years.

Inside the little general store, the crisp scent of

northern Montana pine and the gentle sound of waves sloshing along the shore of Bear Island Lake gave way to the faint smells of leather and cinnamon and the steady tick of the old Coca Cola clock above the cash register.

It all brought back a rush of sepia-toned images from a childhood spent at this lake. Of all the times she and her cousins Laura and Megan, and their best friend, Kris, had sat on the wooden steps just outside, licking melting ice-cream cones as they decided on their next adventure. They'd been inseparable, back then.

The good memories helped settle her nerves. The bad ones she still tried to forget.

Owned by her grandparents, Millie's had always reminded her of a magician's hat. Small as it was, it still held everything from bait to books, from groceries to camping gear and tourist supplies.

Her favorite part had always been the little café set up in the front window, with six wrought-iron, ice-cream tables and an old-fashioned soda fountain complete with eight brass stools that could spin.

And now, this place was her future. Who would've thought? Brimming with emotion, she locked the door behind her and started across the pine-planked floor.

A shadow moved across a beam of moonlight at the back of the store.

She froze, the nape of her neck prickling.

The ticking of the clock slowed.

The glass-fronted pop-and-beer-cooler compressor hummed louder as she strained to listen. A sixth sense told her that the shadow had not been her imagination.

Holding her breath, she edged backward toward the front door, her heart pounding against her ribs and her palms damp.

Ten feet to go.

Five.

She reached blindly behind her for the dead bolt, not daring to turn around.

Had the intruder heard her come in? How fast could she escape? But what then?

The surrounding campgrounds and rustic cabin resorts were empty, now that the tourist season was over. The closest year-round business was a sporting-goods store at least a half mile away that wouldn't open until midmorning.

And with her bad ankle, the chances of outrunning anyone over the age of six weren't good. *God—I need some help here.*

From the back room came the sound of something scraping against the floor...and was that the rasp of a harsh, indrawn breath?

Fear washed through her, turning her knees weak, as she fumbled with her car keys.

The back door squeaked.

Closed with a soft snick of the latch.

Which meant the intruder had left. Or did it? If she ran to her car, he could be out there. Waiting.

But if he was still inside, lying in wait for her, it could be hours before anyone noticed signs of a struggle.

Even if some early morning coffee drinkers peered through the front window, they wouldn't be able to see the back of the store. And no one would even think to stop by until the store opened at seven, anyway.

Tell me what to do, Lord—go, or stay?

Her gaze fell on the old-fashioned desk telephone on the counter behind the cash register, then to the locked cabinet beneath, where she'd stored her grandfather's Korean War–era pistol.

A sense of calm settled over her.

The old keepsake had been like a security blanket, given the iffy Denver neighborhood she'd lived in before sharing a condo with her friend Ashley, but she'd only brought it to this sleepy little town as a memento.

She crept to the register. Quietly she snagged the phone and pulled it down into her lap to dial 911. While whispering to the operator, she fingered through her ring of keys to unlock the cupboard and retrieve the gun.

And then, she moved into the shadows behind a display of fishing tackle and began to pray.

* * *

For the past three months Jack Matthews had slept fitfully at best. He'd greeted the dawn bleary-eyed too many times to count.

But last night he must have finally fallen asleep, because when Max screamed just before dawn, he'd launched out of bed and spun around, disoriented, sure this scream was just one of the many that filled his nightmares.

Then Max had cried out again.

Jack's brain cleared, and he'd stumbled down the dark, unfamiliar hall to the other bedroom of the rental house, where his five-year-old nephew was sitting bolt upright in bed, the blankets twisted around him, his eyes wide and frightened and streaming tears.

No wonder, given the crimson wash of patrol-car lights spinning across his bedroom walls and the male voices drifting up from the road.

Despite Jack's best efforts at trying to comfort him, Max had been awake since then, shell-shocked and subdued after his sobs finally subsided.

It had been a long trip up here from Lawrence, Texas, with too little sleep and three days on the road. Especially while he was still trying to learn how to be a daddy to an emotionally damaged child, who often withdrew from the gentlest hug.

A child who'd rarely smiled since the night he'd watched his parents die.

If he'd still been on speaking terms with God, Jack would have been praying. But if God hadn't chosen to spare the lives of two of the sweetest, kindest people on the planet, why would He care about their grieving, traumatized son?

By all rights Jack, not Janie and her husband, Allen, should've been driving his vintage Mercedes to the gala fundraiser in downtown Dallas.

And it should've been Jack lying in that pretty little cemetery up in the foothills.

Shelving his melancholy thoughts, Jack wearily settled across the kitchen table from Max with a strong cup of coffee in his hand and smiled. "More Cheerios?"

The little boy pushed a piece of cereal across the lake of milk in his bowl, then poked it with the spoon and shook his head.

"I thought you liked Cheerios."

Silence.

Could a five-year-old live on three bites of cereal and one nibble of toast? Despite coaxing and attempts at bribery, he'd only accepted Cheerios and cheeseburgers since they'd left Texas, and even then he'd only take a few bites.

Evidence of just how wrong a choice Jack was for the child's guardian, but there was no one else left— and certainly no one else who loved him more.

"If you aren't hungry, let's go next door to meet our landlord."

Darting an uneasy, sideways glance at him, Max slid off his chair and focused on the buttons of his Sponge Bob pajamas.

"We'll look for something interesting in the store. Some new storybooks, maybe?"

With an almost imperceptible nod, the little boy shied away from the offer of Jack's hand, but dutifully pulled on his clothes and followed him out onto the broad front porch, down the flagstone walk to the road and over to the rustic, one-and-a-half-story log building next door. Millie's Provisions appeared to be a small general store, and the aroma of fresh-baked rolls wafted through the front screen door.

Incredible rolls, from the rich caramel-and-cinnamon scent of them.

Seeing the guarded, hopeful look Max darted at him, Jack felt his heart lift. If it took caramel rolls to see the worry and fear ease in the little boy's eyes, they'd be here with bells on every single day.

"Are you hungry now?" he teased, waggling one eyebrow—a move that had once made the child giggle.

Max regarded him with somber eyes, but he did start up the broad wooden steps to the covered boardwalk running across the front of the building. The effect was straight out of a 1940s Western movie, with pine benches and wooden rockers lining the full length of the storefront, perfect for old folks to gather.

But instead of Montana-cowboy memorabilia,

crossed fishing poles had been hammered to the outside wall, along with an immense fish carved out of wood.

Max stared at the gaping jaws of the fish and stumbled backward, reaching for Jack's hand. "He's *big*."

"That's Edgar." The soft, sympathetic voice came from inside the building. "He scared me until I started fifth grade. But he's really only a big ol' piece of wood."

Jack followed the sound of the voice to a hazy silhouette on the other side of the screen door.

A second later the woman pushed the door open and bent down to smile at Max. "Once I named him Edgar, he didn't seem so scary."

She'd appeared to be of ample size when viewed through the screen, but now he realized that she was about as substantial as Tinkerbell—just a delicate little thing, swathed in a voluminous apron.

In her late twenties or early thirties at most, with long, dark blond hair braided and pulled through the back of a red Millie's Provisions ball cap, she had a smudge of flour on one cheek.

Her light blue eyes sparkled with amusement when she looked up at Jack, and he realized he'd been staring.

"I'm Erin, the owner. I'm running behind in the kitchen, but just give a holler when you finish shopping and I'll zip over to the register."

He'd researched long-term vacation lodging on the

Internet, and the place he'd found here, just a single rental house set in the mountains of western Montana, sounded perfect as a quiet getaway. He'd immediately arranged a lease on the phone.

He'd had to supply multiple references—which he knew she'd verified—and he'd had to pay two months' rent with a certified check before she agreed to a three-month lease and mailed him a key.

Given all that, he'd guessed that his temporary landlady would be tough to deal with should anything go awry, but now his preconceptions melted away.

Once upon a time, he might have felt an instant flash of attraction. He might have even flirted a little, just to see where things led.

But not anymore.

Romance and the responsibilities of single parenting—especially in his case—were mutually exclusive. His ex-fiancée's resentment and abrupt defection after Max's arrival into his life had made that crystal clear.

Worse, Max had inadvertently overheard part of Elana's declaration about not wanting to raise someone else's child. He'd become even more withdrawn after that, and Jack would never risk that kind of harm again.

He offered his hand. "I'm Jack, and this is Max, my nephew."

"I saw the lights go on at the house late last night and went out to check the license plate on your car to be sure it was you, but figured I'd wait until today to come over. And then, well, things got a little busy over here."

Her cheerful smile wavered as she dusted her hand against her apron and accepted a brief handshake, then playfully shook Max's hand, as well. "I'm so sorry I didn't make it over to greet you, too."

Surprised that the child didn't shy away from her touch, Jack nodded toward an immense calico cat curled up on a chair at the end of the porch. "Will she let Max pet her?"

Erin laughed. "Pet her. Lug her around. She came with the store and she's definitely not very energetic."

After Max headed for the cat, Jack lowered his voice. "You had some trouble over here early this morning."

The woman's cheerful facade slipped for a second before she retrieved another bright smile. "Nothing major."

This was a subject he didn't want to discuss with Max at his side, and the child could be back any second. Jack curbed his impatience. "There was a squad car parked in front of this store, with at least two officers and several onlookers. Sounds sort of major to me."

Erin bit her lower lip. "I came into the store to start baking and thought I heard an intruder leaving. I didn't actually *see* anyone."

"What about the cash register? Your merchandise?"

"The cash register was fine. As for the merchandise…" A faint blush tinted her cheeks. "I took over the store a couple of weeks ago, and I've mostly been painting and stocking, getting ready for reopening today. Nothing seems to be missing. And I'm not *absolutely* certain I heard an intruder."

He caught the fine trembling of her hands and an uneasy flicker of her gaze toward the back of the store. "Except?" he asked.

"Nothing, really. Just a feeling…as if things were slightly out of place. But if someone actually did break in, why wouldn't they grab the cash? Or the pricey jewelry and digital cameras in the glass display case by the register?"

"True."

"In the back there are syringes and basic pharmaceuticals stocked for the ranchers and horse owners who treat their own animals. I did inventory on those things a few days ago, so I know none of them were touched. I could tell that the officers who showed up thought I was wasting their time."

Jack thought about Max's terror last night. Dense, dark pine forest loomed over the store, the rental house next door and the cottage out back. Here and there, a twinkling flash of blue revealed the southwest shore of Bear Island Lake beyond the trees. Though it was probably a bustling area in the summer, he hadn't noticed any other houses or other businesses close by.

Anyone could find easy cover out here. They could even approach via the lake to avoid being seen on the highway.

"If nothing was taken, maybe someone has a more personal reason to break in."

"I haven't lived up here since I graduated from high school. I can't imagine who it could be."

She managed to present a casual air, yet now he saw a flicker of fear in her eyes, noticed the way she jammed her trembling hands into the pockets of her apron.

Maybe she was trying to deny it even to herself, but Jack thought she was sure there had been someone here…

And she had an idea who it could be.

TWO

At the end of her first day of business Erin wearily checked the dead bolt on the front door, tallied the cash and checks in the cash register then prepared the money bag and deposit slip.

She moved to the back of the store, then opened the door to the kitchen and flipped on the lights to survey the room before stepping inside.

In every shadow she imagined an intruder. Coiled muscles. Narrowed eyes.

Waiting.

Waiting.

Waiting until no customers were around who could hear her scream.

But no one was lying in wait for her, and this morning's moment of panic had probably been her imagination, as well, not born of a flesh-and-blood threat.

It wouldn't be anything new. Frightening images

had been a part of her dreams for fifteen years, because sweet, giggly, impetuous Laura had likely actually *lived* every terrible second of Erin's nightmares during her last moments on earth—until her captor sliced her throat and buried her before her body was even cold.

Years of counseling and prayer and determination had helped Erin move on, into college and a career and even some romantic relationships, though they were doomed from the start. She'd never been able to forget. Laura's killer had made sure of that.

But she was done running from her past, a past branded by fear and grief and faith that hadn't been strong enough. *God, I know you're with me…that I can trust in You.*

Taking a steadying breath, she stepped into the kitchen and lingered in front of the upright freezer, debating before pulling out five pounds of premium, apple-smoked bacon to thaw in the fridge overnight.

Early September marked the waning of the tourist season, though a few travelers usually filtered north to enjoy the glorious fall colors. But even this first weekend of the month had been slow. Of course, maybe the word had spread when the store was closed for a few months. But even so, there'd been just a handful of customers all day.

She'd recognized only two of them—Martha, the silver-haired postmistress who had been in town since the Dark Ages, and Isabelle Jane Swanson, an elderly, overweight retired schoolteacher who'd been a lifelong friend of Grandma Millie's.

The other customers had been unfamiliar and mostly male, and she'd felt an inward shiver every time one of them walked in the door.

Anyone could stop in on the pretext of buying a fishing lure or a pack of gum. Case the place. Come back after dark. Evil could be hidden behind a casual smile and a bit of innocuous conversation.

Oh, Grandpa Pete, maybe I shouldn't have come back here, after all.

But Gramps was now living in Florida with his elderly sister, finally enjoying life after too many hard, lonely years of running the store by himself, and those were words she would never say to him. He'd come back in a flash and insist on tearing up the contract she'd signed. He would give up his last chance at happiness for her, and that was something she would never allow.

She was grown up now.

Fifteen years had passed since Laura's death, and almost ten since Erin received the last of the eerie, anonymous notes that had arrived every year on the anniversary of the murder. *DON'T TELL.*

Don't tell what? Erin hadn't seen or heard anything that could help with the case, but those ongoing messages had haunted her dreams for years.

Kris and Megan had received them, too, until the murderer apparently committed suicide in an isolated cabin while the sheriff and his deputies were closing in on him. A note with the body confessed to a number of murders—in the sort of grisly detail only the real killer would know.

God was all-powerful, and He granted grace and forgiveness to His children. Erin still clung to the power of faith.

But no matter how hard she tried, she could not forgive the ruthless animal who had stolen Laura's future and the innocence of her best friends with that one, savage act.

The investigators had closed the case. But that hadn't stopped her nightmares or eliminated her fear of being alone outside at night…where shadows loomed and coalesced into frightening specters that threatened to leap out and drag her away. For years she'd felt her heart pound and her palms go damp if she had to cross a darkened parking lot.

I'm finally beyond that now, God. It's all in the past.

"But tomorrow," she muttered to herself, "I'm definitely getting a dog."

The phone rang shrill and loud.

Startled, she spun around on her heel and caught the edge of a saucepan with her elbow. It crashed to the floor, bouncing and rolling drunkenly. The deafening noise reverberated through the store even as she picked up the receiver.

The voice on the line was one she hadn't heard in a long, long time. *"Megan?"*

"Believe it or not." Her cousin's husky laugh brought back a flood of memories of the childhood they'd shared. "I'm not the best at keeping in touch."

"No kidding. I haven't heard from you since last Christmas."

"With all the cutbacks, we're down to just three full-time deputies. The overtime is great, but I've pretty much given up on a personal life. I couldn't believe it when I got your note about moving back to Montana, by the way. I didn't think that would ever happen."

"I'm glad to be here." Erin hesitated. "It took me a lot of years to even entertain the thought, but it was time. And it was good timing for Gramps, too."

"He should've retired a long time ago. But like everyone else in this family, he's just too independent and stubborn for his own good."

"So how about you?" Erin forced a teasing note into her voice. "Are you still busy being the scourge of the bad guys in Marshall County?"

"Until my last breath."

And from the steel in those words, Erin knew it was true. "Would you have even dreamed of being a cop if Laura hadn't died?"

"Maybe not. But every person I put behind bars

makes me feel…well, like I'm doing something for her." Megan gave a self-conscious chuckle. "Crazy, isn't it?"

"That night changed us all. Krissie married too young—"

"To the wrong guy."

"So true. And I moved far away as soon as I could. But you—you turned into the family's superhero."

"A deputy in a sparsely populated county hardly qualifies for that, hon," Megan said dryly.

"From what little you've told me over the years, I think it does. You take way too many risks."

"It's my job. So how's the store? Do you have it up and running again?"

Erin smiled at Megan's swift change of topic. "Yes, but things are pretty slow. I do have someone renting the house, though, to help with expenses."

"So it's all good, then."

"Not exactly. I…um…think I might have had an intruder."

"When?" Megan's voice instantly transformed to cop mode.

"Early this morning. I went inside to start baking and thought I heard someone."

Megan ticked through a dozen probing questions, her voice laced with concern. "So what are your plans for improving security at that place? I'll bet an eighty-year-old granny could kick through that front door."

"I'm going to check on security systems, and I'll look into getting a steel entry door for the back. I'm also thinking about getting a dog."

"Good idea." Megan said briskly. "An adult dog, one with a big bark. I think there's still an animal shelter up in Battle Creek."

"I'll definitely check it out."

"I can guess what you're thinking." Megan hesitated, then her voice gentled. "Given those anonymous notes we all got after Laura died, you might be wondering if her killer is somehow still alive. If he's now coming after you."

Erin stilled.

"I looked into our old case when I first took this job. The guy really did die in that cabin. The fingerprints matched. He's no longer out there watching us…trying to scare us into silence. So don't get spooked over that break-in. hear? Forget it and move on."

Dear, forthright Megan, who'd never been daunted by any challenge in her life. Who always knew what to say, no matter what. "I know. But it's still good to hear a reminder."

Something crackled in the background. Erin could hear the muffled words of a dispatcher—probably on the patrol-car radio.

Then Megan came back to the phone. "I've gotta go—there's an accident out on the highway, and we're short-handed. Take care, you hear? Let's plan on Christmas together, okay?"

"Definitely." Erin cradled the receiver, wishing Megan wasn't several hours away. She remembered the golden days of the childhood summers they'd spent together, when the only worries were cloudy skies and the looming first day of school.

But Megan was right. Coming back to Montana might have briefly revived Erin's old fears, but the past was over. With improved security measures and a noisy dog, she'd be perfectly fine.

And nothing—not old memories and not some two-bit vandal—was going to stand in her way.

Erin set her alarm an hour earlier than usual, finished a batch of fragrant caramel rolls and left a note on Millie's front door saying she'd be open at ten.

By air, the trip to the small town of Battle Creek might've been ten miles at the most. But with the foothills rising into the steeper grades of the mountains, the trip involved thirty-six miles of winding road through a breathtaking example of God's glorious hand.

In Battle Creek, a touristy village of fifteen hundred, she hung a right at the single major intersection in town and drove along the boulder-strewn shore until she spied a faded sign for the Bear Island Lake Rescue Shelter.

As a child, she'd come here with her parents to look at the puppies and kittens. Then, with crisp, white paint and a squadron of volunteers, the place had been impressive to a young girl eager to select a new pet.

Now, the paint was faded and peeling, the chain-link fences sagged with age and the dog runs were choked with weeds. Had the shelter moved to new quarters sometime during the years she'd been gone?

With a sigh, she started a three-point turn. Maybe someone in town would know—

At a flash of movement by the kennel building, she hit the brakes.

"Wait!" A tall, vaguely familiar woman waved to Erin as she jogged across the parking area. "Can I help you?"

If it had been a man headed her way in this lonely and desolate place, Erin would've kept going. Fast. But the middle-aged woman's face was open and friendly, and with a bandanna tying back her hair and the dirt smudge on her cheek, she looked as if she'd been hard at work.

"I should've called ahead," Erin admitted. "I just assumed the shelter would still be open."

"The place closed three weeks ago. Most of the animals have been sent to shelters in the surrounding counties."

Erin sagged against the back of her seat. "There aren't any others in Latimer County?"

"Nope. And this place, as you can see, has gone to ruin. Our county funding dried up, and keeping it going with donations was impossible. Today I'm picking up the last few animals so I can padlock the doors. I was the director, by the way. Polly Norcross."

Erin accepted the woman's brief handshake through the window of her SUV. "What do you have left?"

"A few hard-luck cases. An old, sick collie. A diabetic cat. And Charlie."

As if on cue, a haunting, mournful howl rose from the kennel that made the hair lift at the back of Erin's neck.

"And that's him."

Erin sat up straighter. "He sounds *huge*."

Polly nodded. "He will be, which is a big strike against him with prospective owners. That and all the hair."

"What on earth is he?"

"We think he's Great Pyrenees, with a dash of Bernese mountain dog and maybe a little border collie. He's around seven months old and he's already above knee-high and at least fifty pounds. With all that hair, he looks even bigger, and he's… um…just a tad rambunctious."

"Is he mean?"

"Anything but. Though he does tend to bark incessantly when outside, and he wants to maul people with sloppy kisses. He mysteriously appeared at our door just a couple weeks ago, tied to the fence with twine and thin as a rail."

Erin's heart lifted. Big. Noisy. Friendly. He sounded perfect. "Can I meet him?"

"Maybe when he gets to the Marshall County shelter. I can't process any more adoptions here, because we're closed."

"But if he isn't adopted, then he eventually could be put down?"

"Sadly, yes."

"While you have an eager person right here? Can I just see him?"

"Well…"

"I've just moved back to the area, and I live alone. I really need a dog for companionship, and I like that he'll be big."

"You're from the area?"

"I'm Bill and Jan Cole's daughter. I grew up in—"

Polly's face blanched. "Lost Falls. I babysat your cousins when I was in high school."

Erin studied the woman, and again felt a vague sense of recognition. "It's been such a long time…"

A shadow crossed Polly's expression. "I was Laura Warner's neighbor."

Even after fifteen years, connecting with someone who was part of that terrible past had the power to suck the air from Erin's lungs. "I…I still think about her so often."

"A child's death is so devastating. And when it's someone close to your own age, well…it's something that changes you forever." Polly rested a comforting hand on Erin's shoulder.

"Without a doubt."

"Makes it harder to be alone, too." Again, Charlie's mournful howl sounded from inside the dilapidated building, but this time, Polly gave Erin a long, measuring look. "Every time I hear a noise at night, I jump. I still have an obsession over crime reports on the news."

Erin nodded. The knowledge that life could be snuffed out in an instant—with just the happenstance wrong turn, or wrong encounter—was a hard lesson when one was young and blissfully naive. She sighed as she firmly shelved the memories and dredged up a smile. "I'd better let you finish here. Thanks for your time."

"You know, I haven't been on the payroll for the last month, because there was barely enough money for dog food," Polly mused aloud. "So technically, I'm just a concerned volunteer. If you'd like to meet Charlie, maybe we can work something out."

"Well, buddy," Jack said with a smile. "Looks like another beautiful day. What do you think of this place?"

"'Kay." Max looked up from a pile of Lego blocks on the hardwood floor, his eyes brimming with tears. "I want Mommy here. And Daddy, too."

"Me, too, buddy. Me, too." Jack eased down onto the floor next to him and opened his arms to welcome the boy into his lap for a comforting hug, but Max just bowed his head and stared down at the Lego piece in his hand.

Jack's heart twisted as he realized that he needed a hug as much as Max did, but still didn't know how to reach past the child's wall of lonely grief. He reached for a couple of yellow blocks and snapped them together. "Can I help you make something?"

"A barn?" Max rubbed at his eyes with the back of his hand. "And a truck?"

"You bet." Jack started putting pieces together, forming first a red truck, then a barn in yellow, while Max worked on something that looked like a tower.

Their second night here had been better than the first, without any dramatic interruptions from the store next door. Max had awakened just once but then went back to sleep, and he'd even slept until ten this morning.

Jack, on the other hand, had stared at the gnome-like swirls and knotholes in the pine paneling of his own room until almost dawn.

In the old days, he'd been able to turn his worries over to God and had felt an abiding sense of peace no matter what was going on in his life, but that sure wasn't working anymore.

Janie and Allan's car accident, coupled with the

problems back at his investment company, seemed beyond the realm of faith.

"I have to work on the computer for a while today," he said as he finished a crude approximation of a barn. "Would you like to go next door for some breakfast first?"

Max looked up from the colorful castle he'd started building. "Sticky rolls?"

"Ahh, the caramel rolls. Maybe we can split one after you have something a little healthier." Jack tousled the boy's hair. "I think the store has movie rentals, so maybe you can pick out something to watch while I'm working this morning. Does that sound okay? And then we'll go have some fun this afternoon."

Max nodded.

The child looked angelic, with his pale blond curls and those bright blue eyes framed in long, dark lashes. So angelic and broken and lost that once again a familiar pain settled in Jack's heart like a heavy, cold weight.

Would Max ever again be the happy little boy who'd once romped through his parents' home, innocent of every terrible thing life had to offer? Was it even possible?

Max dutifully got dressed and followed Jack to the store. Again, the warm aroma of caramel rolls wafted through the door as they stepped inside, along with the smoky-sweet scent of bacon.

This time, three of the six small tables in the tiny café area were filled. The other patrons—burly, older fellows who didn't look comfortable in the fanciful, wrought-iron chairs—were bent over steaming cups of coffee, talking about elk hunting and the tinder-dry conditions up in the high country.

As one, their attention swiveled to the newcomers and they nodded in greeting before falling back into their respective conversations.

Jack rested a hand on the boy's thin shoulders. "Wow, I'm hungry. How about you?"

Max nodded silently as he climbed into a chair at the table by the front window.

A moment later, Erin backed through the swinging doors leading into the kitchen, bearing five plates stacked up her arm. She faltered when she noticed Jack, then bustled about delivering the food and filling coffee cups.

She seemed to be working alone and was falling behind, so Jack settled back in his chair and surveyed his surroundings.

The store was actually a large log cabin of sorts, charming and touristy, with rustic beams inside and a soda fountain that looked like it dated back to the 1920s.

The rest of the place seemed crammed with everything under the sun. Even Max appeared to be fascinated, though now his attention was caught by the massive moose head mounted over the soda fountain.

A few dusty Christmas-tree ornaments, remnants from last year, hung from its antlers.

When she arrived at the front table at last, a pad and pencil in her hands, Erin's smile was less friendly than it had been the day before. "Can I help you?"

Jack conferred with Max one more time, then ordered two bacon-and-egg specials, plus caramel rolls in a box to go.

Erin turned his coffee cup upright and filled it, then spared a more genuine smile for Max before she sped back into the kitchen, where she was clearly doing double duty as the cook.

He stared after her for a moment, weighing the possible reasons for her change of attitude. Maybe she was just stressed and busy...but he had a feeling it was something more. "Hey, buddy, want to play hangman? Tic-tac-toe?"

Max shrugged, so Jack started a game of tic-tac-toe on a paper napkin, careful to avoid the best positions on the grid. By the time their food arrived, they'd finished a dozen games and Max had fixed Jack with an accusing glare.

"You didn't try."

Jack grinned. "Nope—you're just really tough to beat."

Max's chin lifted at a stubborn angle eerily reminiscent of Janie's when Jack and his sister were growing up. "Mommy tries. That's better."

Jack's heart caught at the boy's use of the present tense when he spoke of his mother. "How about I try harder next time?" Jack glanced at the bookshelves filled with board games and old paperbacks by the potbellied stove in the corner. "Or we could try Scrabble or checkers."

Max poked at his egg without answering, and Jack belatedly realized that those games were too advanced. "I think I see Candy Land over there, too. Would you like to play that?"

Silence.

Erin appeared at their table again, coffeepot in hand. "Maybe he'd like to ride a horse. There's a stable a mile up the road. Gentle horses and ponies, easy trails for the kids."

Max looked up at her.

"I think I recall a pretty little paint pony just about your size." She grinned. "And I've got someone for you to meet, if your uncle has a minute."

"A *horse?*"

"Nope. But he'll end up the size of a pony someday. I picked up a half-grown pup at the county shelter this morning, and I bet he'd love to play with you."

Max's eyed widened, and seeing his face light up made Jack's heart swell in his chest. "Thanks, Erin. Great ideas." But when she shifted her gaze to meet his, again he felt the temperature in the room drop ten degrees.

Her level look seemed to arrow right through him. "I need to talk to you for a few minutes. Alone."

"Is something wrong?"

She glanced at the other customers, then bent low to whisper in his ear. "I just need to ask you a few questions…or I'm afraid my cousin will be pulling up in her patrol car to take care of it herself. And believe me, you don't want to tangle with her."

THREE

There was no one to watch Max during a private conversation, but there was no way Jack wanted to put this off, either.

Damage control had been his mantra for the past six months, and the faster difficult situations were handled, the better.

And now Max, who'd been all too aware of the reporters, and the baleful glances of people on the street back in Texas, was watching him with very curious eyes. "Were you bad, Uncle Jack?"

Judging by the faint blush rising on Erin's face, she hadn't thought the boy would overhear.

Jack grinned. "I sure hope not. I wonder—maybe we could go see that puppy when we're done here?"

Glancing around the little café, Erin nodded. "The others are nearly done. I can join you in fifteen minutes or so—out back, at the cottage?"

* * *

Embarrassed, Erin fled to the kitchen and ran a load of dishes through the commercial dishwasher, glancing out into the café every few minutes.

When the last customer finally finished and paid his bill, she hung a Back In Ten Minutes sign on the front door and went out to her cottage.

Max was crouched over an anthill, obviously fascinated by the activity. Jack leaned against the porch railing of her cottage, looking tall, dark and—now she knew—mysterious. He watched with razor-sharp intensity as she approached. The air of a predator studying its prey.

After all the years of being so careful, just how foolish had she been in allowing a stranger like this one into her life? Little Max had disarmed her completely, but even evil men had children. She just had to hope Jack wasn't one of them.

She went inside the cottage and collected the pup from its kennel, then brought it out on a leash that she handed to Max. "Here he is. A big, goofy, awkward puppy. But he's very sweet."

Max's eyes rounded. "He's big!"

"And just look at those feet," Erin said. "He's around fifty pounds at seven months. He'll probably end up close to a hundred by the time he's through."

She'd wanted a fully grown, imposing dog with a big bark, but she'd fallen in love with his thick, fluffy white body, coupled with the crescents of tan above his eyes that formed expressive eyebrows. "Want to play with him? He'd love the attention."

Clearly delighted, Max started running about the small chain-link-fenced yard surrounding the cottage. The dog romped alongside him, its white plume of a tail wagging gaily.

As soon as they were out of earshot, Jack turned to face Erin. "So what's up?"

This was going to be so hard, and the words she'd silently rehearsed a few moments ago slipped away. She took a deep breath. "One of my cousins is a deputy in the next county. I told her about having a new boarder, and she called me back late last night."

Jack held her gaze without so much as a flicker. "And?"

"Well, I know you gave me references and all, but Megan is probably the most determined person I know. She insisted that I ask you a couple of questions." Erin rolled her eyes. "If I don't, she'll make the trip and ask you yourself—and I'm afraid she can be a tad abrasive."

"Fire away."

"What brought you to Lost Falls?"

"I thought Max needed time away from the neighborhood he associates with his late parents. And frankly, I needed to get away, too." He shrugged. "I figured the mountains would be a great destination, so I did some research on the Internet and here we are."

Erin nodded. "Megan was just a bit concerned, since there was a break-in the same night you arrived."

Jack's mouth twitched. "If you'd been in that car with Max and me for all those hours coming north, you wouldn't even ask if I had the energy for anything else."

"And…I had some hang-up calls last week before you came."

He laughed at that. "Why would you think I had anything to do with those calls? Did you see my area code on the caller ID?"

Erin felt her neck warm. "I…don't actually have caller ID yet."

"So someone seems to be targeting you, and I showed up at the wrong time. I can understand Megan's concern, believe me." Realization dawned in Jack's eyes. "And that's why you got the dog?"

"Partly for security, though I've wanted one for ages and wasn't allowed to at my old condo in Colorado." She couldn't quite meet his eyes. "There's just one other thing."

He rested an elbow on the railing and leaned back, hooked a heel of his hiking boot on the steps and silently waited.

"Megan did a search of the NCIC criminal database."

"I'm sure she found a lot of hits there," he said dryly.

"None. But…um…I did." Now she felt the

warmth rise to her face. "When I did an Internet search on your name."

She expected a flash of guilt. Perhaps an angry or defensive retort. The look of resignation and sorrow on his face took her by surprise.

"So you read about my investment firm, then." He searched her face. "And about my business partner? It was in the papers for months, so it's certainly no secret."

"I…only know what I read in the online newspapers."

"I'll be glad to fill you in." Jack stared at the child playing with the puppy at the far end of the yard, and lowered his voice. "The past six months marked the end of almost everything in my life that mattered. I lost my only sister and her husband—who were also my closest friends. The reputation of my firm came into serious question, and my business partner, Ted, proved he'd never been a friend at all. Oh, and my fiancée, Elana, found it all just a little overwhelming, so she split."

Erin fought the urge to give him a long, comforting hug. "That's *awful.*"

"The only good thing is that I have Max, though honestly, he deserves better than a single guy without a clue." Jack's smile didn't reach his eyes. "And maybe it was best to find out about Elana's character early on, though less dramatic circumstances would have been nice."

The enormity of what he'd been through nearly took her breath away. "What happened? With Ted, I mean."

"You want to hear my version?" He gave a wry laugh. "That's a first. People back home liked the slanted newspaper articles a whole lot better."

"The press got it wrong?"

"Ted and I were partners for fifteen years. I thought we were as close as brothers. He managed his own accounts, and I managed mine, so I didn't know what he was up to until the day he disappeared with a half-million dollars of his clients' money." Jack's mouth flattened to a hard, determined line. "Many of them were elderly, and he'd been managing their retirement funds."

She'd read the newspaper articles online, which had subtly implicated Jack, though he'd never been arrested and charged. The reporters had made a good point, though. In such a small firm, how could he have been unaware of his partner's dealings? Or had he been involved, and simply better at hiding his tracks?

His steady gaze and the raw pain in his voice told her otherwise.

But the full impact of the theft hadn't hit her until now. "I can't believe anyone would prey on such vulnerable people."

"I can't, either. And I also can't believe my *friend* did it, or that he was spineless enough to commit suicide after he was caught, but it's the truth."

"I...I didn't realize he'd killed himself."

"He was found up near the Canadian border. The investigators are still trying to figure out where he stashed all the money." Jack looked up, his gaze riveted on hers. "I suppose you find me guilty by association, because the press and the people on the street sure did—even though the forensics accountants found absolutely no evidence."

Megan's warnings about renting the house to this man had left Erin feeling uneasy, and she'd barely slept last night. But looking into his eyes now, she saw no cunning, no sly effort to conceal the truth, just soul-deep sorrow, tinged with anger.

"So with Ted gone, there'll never be a trial. No chance to give public testimony about your innocence."

"Exactly. A lot of dry, interminably long reports are filed away someplace that proved it enough to the police investigators." He lifted a shoulder. "But public opinion doesn't easily change. There'll always be those who figure I was crafty enough to get away with the loot."

"So what happens now?"

"I've still got a number of loyal clients and can handle my business via the Internet and phone from up here—at least for a while. But once my lease here is up, I'll have to figure out what to do next...and I have a hunch that moving back to Texas won't be my best choice."

FOUR

"You'll never guess what happened!"

At the sound of Ashley Tompkins's breathless voice on the phone, Erin smiled and leaned against the front counter of the store. They'd been friends since college and had shared Ashley's condo for the past two years. "You were promoted to head nurse?"

"That's a job I *wouldn't* want."

"You found your dream house up in the mountains?"

"Not yet…though the realtor did call about bringing a prospective buyer to see my condo on Tuesday." Ashley took a deep breath. "My car was vandalized in broad daylight last week while it was parked on the street—right out front."

"No way." The condo was in a nice, upscale part of Birch Valley, one of the farthest Denver suburbs. It was a community that prided itself on its safe streets and family environment. "Was there a lot of damage?"

"The lock was jimmied, but the guy must've had trouble getting it open, because he kicked a dent in the door. Then he ripped out the stereo, slashed the leather seats and stole my new GPS."

"Wow."

"You said it. My insurance man said that with the damage and theft, it'll total over two thousand dollars, and my deductible is five hundred." Ashley sighed. "You'd think the vandal would've grabbed the valuables and run, not wasted time slashing my seats."

"A teenager, maybe."

"That's my guess. I just can't believe he got away with it in full view of the windows on the west side of the building."

"Anyone passing by might've assumed the guy was the owner and not looked twice. It sure must've been a shock to go out and see what happened."

"There was one cool thing, though." Ashley's voice turned soft and dreamy. "I'd worked all night at the hospital and got home around eight like always. I'd just had breakfast and was going to turn in when an off-duty cop knocked on my door. He'd noticed something suspicious while driving by, and when he slowed down, the guy in my car took off and ran between the buildings."

"This cop saw the guy? Did he catch him?"

"Nope. By the time he could pull over, the guy was gone, and he was wearing a sweatshirt with the hood pulled up, so his face wasn't visible. Bob called in my license-plate number to find my address so he could come in to tell me."

Erin smiled into the phone. "Bob, eh? Sounds like you got to know this officer pretty well."

"He was a doll. Came right in and sat at my kitchen table while I found my registration papers. Had coffee and everything! And he was really nice about those papers. They were supposed to be in the car glove box, not in my desk."

"You…um…let him in your house?"

"After I saw his badge and ID, of course."

Erin could picture her friend giving a dismissive wave. "Ashley…"

"The ID was real, I know it was." Ashley sighed. "And you wouldn't believe how handsome he was. Late thirties and good-looking in a rugged sort of way. He…he asked if he could call me sometime."

Oh dear. Erin said a swift, silent prayer. Ashley was one of the sweetest people on earth, but at thirty-two she had yet to develop a sixth sense about men who spelled trouble—or if she had it, she blissfully ignored those inner warnings.

"Was he wearing a ring?"

"Of course not!" After a moment's pause, Ashley added, "He really was nice, Erin. He sat a long time over coffee, making a report, and he was concerned about me 'cause I was pretty upset. You know how much I love that car, and that stereo system was the last gift I got from my dad."

"I know." Erin bit her lower lip. "I didn't mean to be so negative. It's wonderful that this cop actually stopped and sought you out. Maybe there's a chance the thief will be caught."

"I hope so." Ashley's voice lightened. "Maybe Bob will stop by again to give me an update!"

"You have to be the happiest crime victim on record," Erin said dryly. "For your sake, I hope this proves to be a godsend."

"Me, too. So how've you been? I haven't heard from you since Linda's wedding."

"I've been terrible about e-mailing and calling these past few weeks. Busy, busy with the move, getting settled and taking over the store."

"Still glad you did it?"

"It was the right thing to do. Gramps is free to enjoy life. I needed a change in mine. I just need to stay afloat financially until the tourist season begins next year."

"With all of your experience managing Phillipe's, you'll do great."

Erin laughed. "Millie's isn't exactly a place for fine dining. I just hope I can appeal to the coffee-and-sweet-roll crowd now." She hesitated over how much to say. "I've had a bit of trouble here, too—and also ended up renting the house to a guy with a questionable past."

"What kind of trouble?"

"A break-in…I think. I heard someone in the store when I went in early on Wednesday. I can't see that anything is missing, so maybe I interrupted him just as he arrived."

"Oh, Erin. You could've been hurt!"

"I was definitely scared—the store is isolated— it's way out by the lake to serve the seasonal crowds. Needless to say, I've already adopted a dog."

"What about electronic security?"

"That's next."

Ashley fell silent. "Are you *sure* you want to stay there? I mean, you could always move back here. Even after the condo sells, we could split expenses on my next place, just like before. You're my all-time favorite roommate."

"Tempting. But I signed this contract. I gave my word."

"Surely your grandfather would let you back out," Ashley protested. "He wasn't convinced you should do it in the first place."

"After just a week? I can't do that to him. He's needed to retire for years, but refused to give up Grandma Millie's beloved house and store. He'd move back in a flash if I called, and then he'd be chained to this place forever. He *deserves* his freedom. And I need to be a big girl about being back here. I probably only imagined there was an intruder, anyway."

Ashley grew quiet. "Are the nightmares back?"

"No—of course not."

"Somehow I'm not believing you. Would it help if I came a little sooner for my visit and stayed awhile? Just until you got acclimated there? I've got some vacation time built up."

"That's sweet of you, but I'm fine. Like I said, the past is…well, it's in the past."

"And what about this bad-news renter dude?"

Erin laughed. "You're still working on the adolescent unit at the hospital, I take it."

"And I love being there…for the most part. I'm going to ask for a permanent transfer to that floor. But you didn't answer my question."

"Jack and his young nephew came up from Texas for a three-month lease. His references checked out okay, but then I found some interesting headlines on the Internet about an investment firm owned by Jack and a partner."

"What did you find?"

"The partner embezzled client funds. Jack says he had no idea that it was going on. Still…"

"Birds of a feather?"

"That was Megan's thought, though he seems like a nice guy. He has a darling little orphaned nephew with him and seems to be a very caring guardian."

"Ahh. I think I hear the sounds of a little interest going on," Ashley teased. "Maybe we've both found someone special."

"Maybe you, but definitely not me. I'm perfectly content to be free, independent and starting my new life—alone."

The initial morning rush—four customers who picked up caramel rolls and coffee to go, their purchases totaling less than twenty dollars—had been over a half hour before Ashley's phone call.

The rest of the morning brought someone wondering if the store carried the *New York Times,* a request for a whole-house aerosol flea bomb and a walk-in customer who dawdled over nearly every display in the store before purchasing a single package of gum.

Disheartened, Erin stepped out the back door and walked the few steps to the gate leading into the yard surrounding the cottage. As soon as she whistled, Charlie bounded across the yard like a massive white mop and threw himself at the gate, his fluffy paws draped over the top rail and his tail wagging madly.

"Ready to come in for a while?" she murmured, resting her cheek against his soft fur. "Best behavior only, though. Understand?"

She lifted her gaze toward the west, where splashes of early September crimson and brilliant gold were already starting to paint the hills rising behind the store, offering the promise of an influx of fall leaf-watchers during the upcoming weekends. *Please, God, let that happen.*

Peak fall color usually hit the first weekend of October, just three weeks away. Would it bring an infusion of tourist dollars or echo the lonesome Labor Day weekend, when the exodus away from the resort area brought almost no tourists into Millie's?

Charlie licked her cheek, interrupting her thoughts. "I wish you were more grown up and a lot bigger," she murmured, giving his shaggy neck a hug.

He wiggled ecstatically, his tail wagging as she snapped a lead onto his collar.

"Can you remember to be good?" She framed his face with both hands and looked into his soulful, dark eyes. "That means no potato chips ever again. No kissing customers. Stay by my side, okay?"

His first shift as a guard puppy hadn't gone well, and if a dog could feel guilt, this one sure did. His brown eyebrows wiggled up and down as he tried to avoid her gaze, and his head dropped lower into her hands.

Only the memory of the torn bags and chips scattered everywhere kept her from laughing at his forlorn expression.

He'd apparently thought the chips weren't only tasty, but were great for dog hockey, because she'd found them in every corner of the store after leaving him alone for the ten minutes it took to run to the post office.

The dog book she'd been reading said an animal couldn't associate a reprimand with a behavior unless the two were nearly simultaneous, but Charlie clearly knew what she'd been talking about.

He trotted to the front of the store at her side, giving the potato-chip display a wide berth, his head averted and his white plume of a tail hanging low.

She motioned to the soft dog bed she'd set up behind the cash register. "Stay."

With a resigned sigh, she turned to the drawers beneath the front counter and searched each of them again. Her extra set of keys for the property had been here, hidden at the back of the top drawer. Or was it the second? She couldn't remember.

Crouching at the bottom drawer, she methodically emptied the contents onto the floor.

Old receipts.

Outdated maps and brochures for area resorts.

A lifetime supply of pens and pencils and stray Band-Aids.

Junk mail Gramps had never bothered to open, though he'd kept it for some reason.

She'd already searched the cottage and the small kitchen at the back of the shop, but to no avail. An uneasy sensation crawled up her spine. *What if the intruder had found those keys?*

She closed her eyes, imagining the quiet snick of a lock in the dead of night. Furtive footsteps sliding across the worn plank floors of the cottage. A rough hand on her shoulder—

"Hey."

The gravelly baritone came out of nowhere. She jerked around, a hand at her throat as she lost her balance and fell against the wall.

Silhouetted by the overhead lights, a man loomed over the counter. His face was cast in shadows and framed by a wild array of long, steel-gray hair. "You open here or what?"

Next to her, Charlie froze and gave a long, low growl.

"O-of course." Flattening her hands against the wall at her side, she slowly straightened without taking her eyes from the man's face.

"Good. I didn't see you back there." He tipped his head toward the door. "Ollie and me would like some of those good caramel rolls and coffee we've been hearing about."

Her gaze veered toward the entrance, where a towering, heavyset man rocked on his heels, fidgeting with the battered cowboy hat he held in front of his waist with both hands.

For all his size, there was a simple, childlike quality in the way Ollie darted a glance at her, then dropped his head to continue staring at his hat.

The man standing at the register looked like an aging hippie, his grizzled face ravaged by the years. With the ripped-off sleeves of his sweatshirt and the heavy tattoos covering his arms, he would've blended in with the homeless old men and druggies who lurked in the dark corners and alleyways of any city, guarding their ragtag possessions.

How had she missed hearing footsteps on the wooden porch outside or the tinkle of the bell over the door? Had she been too lost in thought—or had they slipped quietly into the store, intending to score the cash in the till before seeing she was behind the counter?

Taking a deep breath, she waved a hand toward the café area and wished some other customers would wander in. "Have a seat, and I'll get your coffee."

The man made a sharp hand motion to Ollie, then the two shuffled over to one of the tables and pulled the chairs back with a screech of wood against the plank flooring.

Ollie eagerly grasped his mug between both hands as soon as she poured coffee for him, his wide, pasty-white face a picture of bliss.

"I tried to buy this place from your grandpa for years, but heard you took over for him," the older man growled as he leaned back in his chair and glanced around the store. "It's a shame he didn't do a better job of warning you away."

"Warning me?"

"This place has been struggling for a long time, but it's always worse trying to hang on over the winter without the tourist trade. You won't see many locals, either. When you want to give up, you know who to call."

She tried not to stare. Could he be the guy who had broken in the other night, hoping to frighten her away? "Why would you even be interested, then?"

He shrugged. "Sentiment. I grew up near this part of the lake. I'm Barry Hubble, by the way. We're neighbors."

"We...we are?" Stunned, she imagined a run-down shack littered with beer bottles and a fierce, mangy dog chained to the front door. He definitely didn't look like the sentimental type.

"I own Mountain View Florist—a little less than a mile up the road."

"You're a *florist?*" She tried to quell the incredulity in her voice, but knew she'd failed when she caught the knowing look in his eyes.

"Gifts, floral arrangements, a greenhouse out back. Ornamental bushes, trees...you name it."

"Orchids," Ollie breathed.

Barry tipped his head in acknowledgment. "Those are his favorites. You help me out sometimes, don't you, Ollie?"

The other man nodded earnestly.

The incongruity of Barry's appearance, manner and his supposed profession made alarm bells go off in her head.

Florist or not, there was something about him that

she couldn't quite trust, and his friend appeared devoted enough to do anything he was asked without question.

Charlie apparently felt the same way. He furtively moved from behind the cash register, head low and one slow step at a time, his stalk mode revealing some vestige of his border-collar genes.

"Easy, boy." Erin went to him and rested a hand on his head, feeling his low growl vibrate through her fingertips.

His attention didn't waver from corner of the café where Ollie and Barry were seated.

Frowning, Barry swiveled in his chair and leaned back to peer around a greeting-card display. "Bad business, having a dog like that here. He's gonna cause you no end of trouble, with customers and all."

"I like to think he'll be good protection."

"Humph. What you'll have is lawsuits when he bites some kid or scares some old lady into falling over. If I were you," he added darkly. "I'd get rid of him soon as you can."

FIVE

Erin pulled back on Charlie's collar until she broke his rigid attention away from the two men in the café, then led him back to his bed behind the cash register and ordered him to lie down.

Whimpering, he obeyed, but his eyes were still riveted on the front of the store—as if he was waiting for his two enemies to come into view.

"I don't blame you," Erin whispered, leaning down to give him a reassuring stroke. From outside came the sound of a car pulling up to the front of the store. "But it'll be okay."

Erin straightened to greet an older woman who headed toward the coolers along the back wall. After the woman bought a gallon of milk and left, Erin continued her search through the drawers for the heavy ring of keys.

Barry and Ollie polished off several cups of coffee

and a half-dozen caramel rolls—a feat she'd never thought possible.

At the cash register Barry paid the check and studied her for a long moment from beneath his shaggy eyebrows. "It ain't only the slow trade all winter long. Ol' Pete never had much trouble out here. Oh, maybe some shoplifters, but nothing big since 'eighty-nine. But a young gal like you, all alone…" His voice trailed off as he shook his head. "It's just bad business all around. You're gonna need help one of these days, and there just ain't anyone close by."

"Maybe." Behind the counter Charlie shifted and leaned against her legs, his body trembling. "But that's why I got a dog. A fierce one, actually," she added. "Very."

"Looks like a troublesome pup to me." He pulled a business card out of his wallet and flipped it onto the counter. "My business and cell numbers are on the card, in case you ever need any *real* help."

Bold, black lettering spelled out Mountain View Florist against a background of colorful roses and greenery, with lacy white latticework around the perimeter of the card.

The incongruity of the man in front of her and the frilly, feminine design nearly made her smile, though the thought of being alone here at night, with him at her door, made her shiver, instead.

She handed over his change. "Wouldn't I call the sheriff?"

He gave a humorless laugh. "Yep—but out here, don't count on fast attention."

He and Ollie were going out the door when she regained her composure. "Wait—what happened in 'eighty-nine?"

"Some guy came up from California to hit a lot of the resort towns. He knocked your grandpa out cold and ran off with the whole cash register when he couldn't get it open."

Horrified, she put a hand to her cheek. "Grandpa Pete never said a word about that!"

"You just never know what—or who—could be lurking in the shadows. And everyone up here knows how long it takes to get help." He bared his teeth in an eerie smile as he stepped out the door. "Even the bad guys, lady. So think about that."

Jack eyed the pristine white steeple of the old country church, set his jaw, then took Max's hand and walked through the gathering of folks chatting on the lawn outside.

Lost Falls was a small town that undoubtedly served a wide and mostly unpopulated mountainous area, but the people in front of the church all seemed to know each other very well. From the whispers and glances coming his way, he knew they were probably curious about the stranger in their midst.

A few appeared to start in his direction, then seemed to think better of it—perhaps after catching the grim expression on his face.

He made himself smile and nod, though right now he just couldn't bring himself to engage in idle conversation.

Janie and her husband had never missed Sunday church if they could help it, and Jack was certainly going to follow through on their behalf by seeing that Max still went. But even after six months, stepping into a church filled him with a renewed sense of anger. Janie had been a devout Christian, yet where was God on the night of that fatal crash? Why hadn't he protected her?

And if she didn't deserve God's sheltering wing, who did? The blind faith of Jack's youth had been shattered the day she died, leaving an aching, empty place in his heart.

Someone fell in step with him and he glanced over to find Erin Cole giving him an uncertain smile.

"Everything okay?"

"Fine." She looked like a ray of sunshine on this cloudy September day, in her soft yellow sweater-and-skirt set and with all that blond hair cascading down her back, but he quickly reined in his flare of attraction.

Max was his greatest focus, followed by efforts to salvage his business via the phone and Internet. He certainly wasn't in Montana for any sort of romance— short-term or otherwise—no matter how pretty she was.

She tilted her head to study him, her hair shimmering like a silky waterfall over her shoulders. "You look a little…stressed. Is everything all right with the house?"

"Great."

"Did Charlie come?" Max twisted his hand within Jack's as he craned his neck to look around them, then he gave Erin a hopeful look.

She laughed, the sound soft and musical. "I'm afraid this is the last place he should be. He's a sweetie, but he's just a tad rambunctious for this crowd."

"Can we play today?"

"Only if it's all right with your uncle." Erin lifted a brow. "The fenced backyard ought to be pretty safe, though I wouldn't leave them there alone."

Did he look that inept as the boy's guardian? Stung, Jack shot a glance at her. "Of course not."

"Well, then—" her eyes veered toward a trio of ladies by the steps, and she waved at them "—enjoy the service. I haven't been here in decades, but if Pastor Gordon is still here, I'm sure you'll enjoy it. He's an amazing preacher and—"

"Doubt that," Jack muttered.

He hadn't meant to say the words aloud, but she must've heard him, because she gave him an odd look. "And you still came?"

Glancing down, he gave his nephew's hand a gentle squeeze. "It's the right thing to do, eh, Max?"

Erin's stride faltered. "Forgive me. I—I'll talk to you later."

She joined the women over by the steps and fell into animated conversation with them without looking back, and Jack felt strangely bereft at her departure.

Not on a personal level, of course. It was just that adult conversation was in short supply these days, barring the clients he talked to on the phone.

Still, his thoughts veered back to Erin, and he found himself wondering about her previous life in Denver.

How had she managed to stay unmarried all these years? Were the men in Colorado so blind that they hadn't seen her?

Watching her visiting with her friends, her face open and sunny, and her musical laughter floating on the breeze, he was suddenly glad—even if he *wasn't* interested.

Jack swept Max into his arms and climbed the wide stone steps leading to the open double doors of the church, where the pastor stood in his white robe, his face wreathed in smiles as he greeted each person who entered.

"And who's this?" he exclaimed when Jack

reached the door. He playfully reached for Max's hand to shake it. "Are you bringing your daddy to church, young man?"

Max jerked his hand back, his eyes wide, and sucked in a deep breath as he twisted away and burst into tears. "Not my daddy! He's not!"

"I'm his uncle," Jack said, though the older man probably couldn't hear him over the wailing child. "His parents are recently…gone."

The minister blinked. "I am so sorry. I never meant to upset him."

"Happens a lot," Jack said firmly. "So don't think twice about it. And maybe the church reminds him too much of the funeral." He leaned back to look at Max's tear-streaked face. "I don't think we'd better try going in today. Maybe another time."

He shook the pastor's hand and accepted the man's words of sympathy, then turned and headed back down the stairs. The crowd parted as he strode toward the parking lot with the crying child in his arms.

"I want Mommy," Max said brokenly, resting his damp face against Jack's neck. "I want her back."

"I know you do, sport. I know." Jack rubbed the boy's trembling back. "You know what? I think we should check out those ponies today. Would you like that?"

"P-ponies?"

"Remember? The lady at the store told you about them. It's a nice day to be outside, after all. We'll go home and after lunch, I'll get the directions."

Ponies wouldn't heal a broken heart, but anything to help bring some fun into Max's life was worth it, whatever the cost.

After buckling Max into his car seat, Jack rounded the front of the car and braced his hands on the door frame before climbing behind the wheel.

Fun. What fun did the poor kid have these days? The past three months had been filled with constant turmoil.

The accident.

The funeral.

Closing down Janie's house and storing the contents, the endless legal complications at the abrupt end of a life. And then there was Ted's unbelievable act of greed and the ensuing, rabid attention of the local press. Elana's background as the daughter of a wealthy, influential family had only made it worse.

Through all of it, Max had been pale and shell-shocked and eerily quiet, and only recently had he started to talk more and to cry over the loss of his parents.

Did he need playmates? More toys?

With his August birthday he wouldn't start kindergarten until next year—Jack knew that much—but maybe he needed some sort of preschool where he could interact with other kids?

The next three months could be a long, long time in the poor little guy's life, but maybe Erin would have some ideas or would know someone he could ask.

Erin turned slowly and scanned the store, giving her search one last try. Had she missed anything? Not likely. She'd looked everywhere, high and low, and the keys were gone.

She snapped her fingers. "Come on, Charlie. We've got to let Jack know."

An image of Jack cradling his distraught nephew flashed through her thoughts, and she felt a flash of guilt.

They'd shown up at church, but given his terse comment, she'd had the temerity to actually question why he'd come—as if she'd had any right. *Please, Lord—forgive me for my foolish words.*

Whether or not he wanted to be there, Jack had shown up, hadn't he? Embarrassment warmed her cheeks as she turned to a display of stuffed animals, picked out the right one, then dropped it in a gift bag.

"It's a peace offering," she told Charlie when he sniffed at the bag. "Do you think it will help?"

He cocked his head and looked up at her.

"You're right. The best thing would be a dog just like you. But maybe he'll like it, anyway."

Charlie dutifully trotted at her side as she walked the fifty feet between the front door of the store and the matching log home next door. She found Jack and Max coming down the porch steps.

"Oh," she said, faltering. "I guess you're leaving."

"Actually we were coming over to ask you for directions to that stable."

"To see ponies," Max added.

"I…um…brought you something. Charlie and I picked it out." She offered the gift bag to the boy and held her breath as he pulled out the tissue, then withdrew a floppy, white, stuffed animal that looked a lot like Charlie.

Max's eyes widened as he hugged it to his chest and rubbed his cheek against the thick, soft fur. "Can I keep it? Really?"

"You bet."

"Thank you!" Still gripping the stuffed animal in one arm, he knelt to give Charlie a hug, then pulled on the pup's collar. The two of them trotted up the stairs to the covered porch, where Max pushed a ball across the floor and watched Charlie go after it.

She smiled at the boy's tight grip on the toy. "The stable is north on 29, then left on Three Peaks Road about three miles. Can't miss the sign." She cleared her throat. "Actually I…um…came over to apologize for a couple of things, if you have a minute."

"Apologize?" Jack flashed a quick grin. "I can't imagine what for."

"For being rude at church, of all places." She rolled her eyes. "I can't believe I said what I did."

He laughed. "I'm not sure I can accept an apology when there was nothing to offer it for."

"And I need to apologize for something else—inconvenience. I'm missing a set of keys for all the locks on the property, including the house. I've looked everywhere."

He shrugged. "If they turn up here, I'll let you know. I haven't seen anything, though."

"The thing is, if someone *did* break into the store and those keys have fallen into the wrong hands... well, none of us is safe. So I talked to a locksmith in town. He's going to replace all the locks during the next few days, and he'll be starting with your house this afternoon."

"Do you know if this locksmith is also a handy-man?"

"He dabbles with most anything, so I hear."

"Then do you have a minute?" Jack hiked a thumb toward the entryway on the porch. "I'd like to show you the ceiling fan in the living room."

She followed Jack to the front door. "Max?"

The boy shook his head. "I wanna stay outside with Charlie."

The windows and door were open to the soft September breeze, and she and Jack would be just inside, well within hearing range. "We'll be just a minute. Just don't leave the porch, okay?"

Slipping closer to the house, the watcher stifled a growl of impatience.

Two days.

Two. Whole. Days.

And what had he accomplished? Exactly nothing—and the clock was ticking. With only an hour or so left today there'd no longer be time to go through the house. Especially if the guy and his kid continued to hang around.

And coming back next week might be another big trip for nothing, if that renter was still there.

But a few minutes ago, he'd watched through his binoculars as the man and his kid came out of the house, and it looked like they were leaving. So he'd circled back through the trees, then crept along the side toward the corner of the full-length front porch, just to make sure they were gone—

A twig snapped beneath his foot at the moment he caught sight of the kid sitting cross-legged on the porch, hugging a dog.

Startled, he cursed and pulled back.

It was too late. The boy's head jerked around, his eyes flared wide. His mouth dropped open in obvious terror as he started to push the dog away from his lap.

"No, no—I'm just a friend," the man wheedled. "You sure got a nice dog there. What's your name, kid?"

The kid screamed. A blood-curdling, terrified scream that sent the dog into a frenzy of barking.

It rushed across the porch to throw itself at the rail, its snapping jaws barely missing his face as he fell backward into the bushes.

From inside the house came the sounds of running footsteps. "Max? Max!"

Swearing under his breath, the man raced for cover. He'd be back. He *had* to retrieve what he'd come after, or his life was as good as over.

Settling into a steady jog, the man smiled to himself as he headed for the car he'd parked out of sight a good mile away.

There'd be another day. He *would* succeed. And if anyone got in his way, it would be their own, very unfortunate mistake.

SIX

Erin raced out to the porch after Jack.

Max was huddled in the far corner behind the porch swing, arms wrapped around his knees and the stuffed animal, his eyes closed tight. Charlie was there, too, crowded next to him with his furry head resting on the boy's shoulder.

But oddly, after those terrified screams, the boy was silent—as if he'd taken himself into some other world.

Jack knelt in front of him. "Hey, buddy. What happened? Did you fall?"

The child was so still he might have been carved of marble.

"Were you scared of something?" Jack turned and surveyed the empty porch. "What was it?"

Again, no response.

Erin walked around the perimeter of the porch and studied the surrounding property. Was that a dark shadow off in the distance, moving through the trees? Or just her imagination? Was it a deer?

She looked to the north, but there were no customers parked in front of Millie's, waiting for her to take down the Back In Ten Minutes sign and unlock the door.

And there were no hikers or animals that she could clearly see in the surrounding stand of pines, though with the dense undergrowth, something smaller might be out there. A fox, or maybe a coyote.

Bright September sunlight filtered through the trees. The air was crisp with the scent of pine. A fitful breeze toyed with the thick, powdery ribbon of dirt marking a trail that led off into the forest, raising small, swirling dust devils.

A beautiful day, not a dreary one made for mist and shadows and bogeymen.

"I don't see anything, Jack," she murmured as she came back to stand next to him.

He rested a tentative, gentle hand on the boy's shoulder. "Here—want to come with me? We can sit on the swing and you can tell me why you're scared, okay?"

Charlie anxiously nudged the child's face, looked up at Jack and whined, then paced in a tight circle and lifted his head to stare out at the pines.

When Max still didn't respond, Jack picked him

up in his arms and moved to the swing, where he held the boy on his lap.

"Did you see…a big deer?" Erin asked, sitting next to them. "Or a bear?"

The boy gave Erin a silent, stricken look.

"Hmm. What else could there be? Maybe a moose with bi-i-i-g antlers, like the one in the store?"

Max shook his head, but just barely.

"Someone walking on the trail?"

Instead of snuggling into his uncle's comforting embrace, Max looked as if he were afraid to trust Jack or anyone else. He kept his eyes riveted on her face.

"You know," she continued in a soothing voice, "I looked out there and didn't see anything. But we do see hikers go by occasionally. The trail running behind your house goes on for many, many miles. Did someone come close to your house?"

A faint nod.

She gave him an encouraging smile. "Was it a lady?"

"No," he whispered, choking back a sob.

"Fear of strangers, especially men, has been an issue since…that night." Jack wrapped his arms around the child and met Erin's gaze. "Sometimes he's afraid, but no one is really there. The psychologist thinks it's related to his terror when the EMTs came on the scene."

Erin nodded at his careful choice of words within

the boy's hearing, but the expression on Max's face seemed too stark, too distressed, for this to be over anything imaginary.

Could Barry have come here hoping to stir up trouble? Could he have sent Ollie?

She bent down to try again. "Did the man say anything to you?"

Max turned away from her.

"You know what, I think it's time to go find that pony and have some fun," Jack said. "What do you think, pal? We can always talk later."

Max gave a single nod.

"And when we get back, maybe we can do some more thinking when things are a little calmer." Jack stroked the boy's hair, then glanced at Erin as he stood up and fished his car keys out of his pocket. "Believe me, I want answers as much as you do."

Erin swept the store, then dragged in a ladder from the storage shed in back and began working on the inventory.

Thick dust still covered the more inaccessible merchandise, some of which appeared to have been in place for decades. *Oh, Gramps...you hung on to this place way too long.*

Sentiment over his late wife had probably kept him here, coupled with dread at the prospect of living alone with nothing to do. But the long hours had taken their toll on him, and the weariness in his stooped posture when Erin had kissed him goodbye at the airport was enough to break her heart.

The bell over the door tinkled.

Charlie, who followed her everywhere and tended to lie down within inches of her feet, rose slowly, his tail thumping against the ladder as she climbed down.

"Goodness gracious, you're going to land in the hospital, climbing all over the rafters like that!"

Erin laughed. Without looking, she knew exactly who it was, from the voice and the lemony scent of Jean Naté wafting into the store. "Now, Isabelle, it's not as bad as all that. I was only on a ladder."

"Humph."

A good eighty if she was a day, Isabelle Swanson was a short, rotund woman with a flair for clothes in outrageous color combinations, but she was sharp as a tack and one of the kindest women Erin had ever met.

Erin dusted her hands against her jeans and headed to the front of the store to give her a hug. "You look wonderful, as always." And she did, with her silver curls perfectly coiffed and her bright red coat and lilac dress. "I totally love the silver shoes."

"Never did think pretties had to be saved for evening. My kiddies love them."

"You're still babysitting?"

"Third generation. some of them, bless their little hearts. Not full-time anymore, but it helps fill my days." She waggled a snowy eyebrow. "I saw you in church, but didn't get a chance to say howdy."

"I'm sorry I missed you." Erin gestured toward the café. "I'm ready for a break. Would you like some coffee, on the house?"

"With a chance to visit? My, yes." Isabelle followed her to one of the tables. "It's good to see you back after all these years."

Erin brought out a tray with cups, some cookies and a pot of fresh coffee. "I'm glad to be here. I stayed away far too long."

Isabelle gave her a knowing look. "Sometimes a fresh start is best, when there's been so much sorrow."

"And then sometimes it's best to finally face it all head-on and let go of the past."

"So, do you have a special fella?"

"Nope, and no plans to. either."

"You're too young to be saying that." Isabelle's eyes twinkled. "You might just change your mind when the right one comes along. Like that handsome man renting Pete's house, for instance."

Erin choked on her sip of coffee.

"I've seen him with that boy of his," Isabelle continued. "He seems like a really good daddy."

"He'll just be here for a few months, and then they're going back to Texas."

"Maybe he'll decide differently. He could fall in love with this town. Settle down."

"He's a nice guy and all, but I learned my lessons early on. You might *think* you can change someone, but that doesn't mean you can."

Isabelle chuckled. "I can't see a lot I'd change about that man."

"I think he and I are poles apart in our faith beliefs, though. Such different life views just don't work in the long run."

"I wouldn't jump to any conclusions just yet. He hasn't been up here all that long, has he?"

Erin laughed. "You do keep track of our town, Ms. Swanson."

"Pays to keep up with things. Now about this young man of yours…"

Isabelle was a sweet old lady, but she was still as determined as a pit bull. "Strictly business. I'd like to ask you about someone who was in here over the weekend, though. Ollie?"

"Ah, yes. Sad thing, really. His mother was quite a drinker. I heard he was dropped as a baby and ended up with brain damage of some sort." Isabelle shook her head, remembering. "He should have had special schooling back in the day. But either his parents didn't bother, or he slipped through the cracks in the education system. I'm sure I never saw him in school when I was teaching."

"So he works for Barry? He seems devoted."

"It must be a terribly lonely life for him, otherwise. I hear he still lives by himself in the run-down place where he grew up, and that he adamantly refuses to move into a group home."

"Can't someone help him?"

"The local churches drop off food for him, but other than doing occasional odd jobs, he's a pretty reclusive guy. He won't even open his door to the county welfare people."

"Would he…" Erin carefully chose her words. "Could he be encouraged to do anything illegal? Does he understand the difference between right and wrong?"

Isabelle straightened in her chair. "Why do you ask?"

"Just wondering. I think someone broke into the store one night, and there might have been a prowler outside my house."

Isabelle shook her head. "Ollie might be easily led, but I don't think he'd cause anyone harm. Folks around here try to look after him. He's sort of a town mascot, really. If he got a little mixed up, they'd correct him, not haul him off to jail."

Which didn't exactly answer her question. "And what about the florist?"

"Barry?" Isabelle pursed her lips. "He's been up here for at least ten, fifteen years, but I don't really know him. He keeps to himself, but he's done well with the garden center and flower shop. Not an easy thing these days."

"He warned me about the dangers around here. Yet he looked more dangerous than anyone else I've met since coming back."

"I suppose so, with all those tattoos and the wild hair. I think he must be a relic from the Vietnam War protest and flower-child era. But," Isabelle added thoughtfully, "he does have an amazing green thumb."

The more Erin saw of Jack, the more she was sure that he was an upstanding, honest guy. Thrust into the difficult situation of raising his sister's child, he was doing his best and had shown himself to be a kind and caring man, despite Erin's earlier reservations.

Barry was another story.

She thought about the missing keys, and Max's terrified reaction when he'd been on the porch with Charlie. If Barry was still after Grandpa Pete's property, could he be trying to frighten her into selling out? He certainly lived close enough to keep watch on the place, so he could plan his next move.

"You trust Barry, then?"

"Well…I guess so." Isabelle considered her words for a moment. "One day I bought some daylilies there and mistakenly gave him a twenty, instead of a ten. He followed me clear out into the parking lot to give me my proper change."

Presenting an honest facade could be a cover for other dealings, though. "Would you say this area is safe these days?"

"It's funny you should ask. Miriam Walker was just telling me that she heard about a break-in on her police scanner last week." Isabelle's eyebrows drew together. "I think that was the first bit of trouble we've had all year around here."

"Nothing more than that?"

"This is a safe town, my dear." Isabelle leaned forward and patted her hand. "Don't let old tragedies make you so jumpy. Worrying about everything and fretting about the people around you will just send you to an early grave."

Isabelle's calm, almost patronizing words continued to play through Erin's thoughts long after the old woman left. Lost Falls was a safe town?

Erin had felt the opposite was true for the past fifteen years and had resisted the idea of moving back for that very reason.

God—help me just let the past go and trust that I'll be safe. She believed in God's power and mercy, truly she did. The Bible verse she'd memorized after Laura's death had been close to her heart ever since. How often had she silently recited it, clinging to its powerful message?

Don't worry about anything; instead, pray
about everything. Tell God what you need, and
thank Him for all He has done. If you do this,
you will experience God's peace, which is far
more wonderful than the human mind can
understand. His peace will guard your hearts
and minds as you live in Jesus Christ.

The beautiful words had given her comfort. They'd
made her stronger, and they'd given her peace. Now,
she firmly shelved the old memories whenever they
surfaced, determined to live a full and abundant life
just as God wished for all of His children.

Yet, the subtle threats she'd sensed since coming
here felt *real,* not like something born of her imagination, even though the deputies had clearly thought
she was crying wolf. She'd seen it in their eyes. And
Isabelle was certainly nonchalant.

With a sigh Erin went to work in the kitchen,
cleaning and sanitizing the work surfaces, then
scrubbing the floor until it shone. She glanced at the
clock now and then, wondering how Max's cowboy
adventure was going.

By five she started to worry. Had the little guy
fallen off? Gotten hurt? Maybe Jack and Max were
sitting in the E.R. at the tiny community hospital up
in Battle Creek, waiting for X rays or an orthopedic
consultation. Maybe—

At the sound of a car door slamming, she hurried to the front window of the store to peer out.

Jack's SUV was parked in front of the house. Jack and Max climbed out and lingered for a moment, then headed for Millie's. Max, she saw with amusement, still clutched the stuffed dog as if it might escape.

The two of them came into the store, bringing with them the definite scent of horses and hay. She'd never seen the little boy smile with such complete abandon, and it transformed him into the child he'd probably been before his world fell apart.

"So, how did it go, cowboy?" Bracing her hands on her thighs, she leaned down to his level and reached out to brush away the dust on his cheek. "Did you see the pony?"

"Her name was Fireball," he breathed with reverence. "She was white and brown and had a really, *really* long tail. And she was *fast!*"

"She sounds beautiful. Did you get to ride her?"

Max nodded. "And I didn't fall off."

Erin straightened and saw the amusement in Jack's eyes. "Really fast, huh?"

He rested a hand on the boy's shoulder. "Max not only rode at a walk, but at a trot—while being led in the pony ring. He did a great job. So now we're here because we figured a tired, dusty cowboy might need to mosey over for some ice cream. We're thinking sundaes. Mint chocolate chip, with hot fudge, whipped cream and a cherry."

"Sounds exactly right." She strode over to the soda fountain, washed her hands and began preparing the confections. "There's a restroom in back if you want to wash up."

By the time she finished, they were back and in their customary table at the front window, Max's cheeks and hands glowing pink.

After the first few bites, Max's eyelids started to droop. Minutes later he folded his arms on the table, rested his cheek on them and fell asleep.

Jack pushed Max's dessert toward the center of the table. "I guess being a cowboy is hard work. I wish you could have seen him—it was like having the old Max back again. He was so excited, he was even laughing. I haven't heard him laugh since before the accident."

There were no other customers in the store, so Erin brought a couple of cups of coffee over to the table and pulled up a chair. "Can you take him there again sometime?"

"Definitely." A corner of Jack's mouth lifted. "If I had the right place back in Texas, I'd bring that pony home with us."

"That would be any little boy's dream."

"It seemed to make him genuinely happy for the first time in months. He's been talking more lately, but most of the time he still seems so distant—like he feels totally alone."

At the depth of emotion in Jack's eyes, Erin reached across the table to cover his hand with her own. "But you do so well with him. Anyone can see that."

"On the surface, maybe…but I don't know how to get through to him, not really. Last night he fell over his Lego blocks and scraped his knee. He would've run to Janie or Allen for comfort, but he doesn't ever come to me. He'll go off behind the sofa to cry until I find him."

The image of the child, still struggling so desperately with his grief, made Erin's eyes burn. "He'll come around in time, won't he?"

"The counselor back home said this trip would help us bond, but maybe she was wrong. Maybe it won't ever happen, no matter what." He stared out the window toward the empty highway and the mountains beyond. "If we head for Texas sooner than planned, I'll still pay the full three months' rent."

Texas. Erin felt her heart squeeze. "Why would you go back early?"

"I'm trying my best to make him happy, but I'm starting to wonder if he misses being with other kids, since he was in preschool last year." He gave a deprecating laugh. "And despite the disaster with Ted, I'm still trying to run a business…or what's left of it."

"Is anyone in your office while you're gone?"

"My secretary is more efficient than anyone I know, and she's keeping everything afloat. But the dial-up Internet connection here is slow, and without everything in my own office at hand, I'm not nearly as productive." He lifted a shoulder. "Every day she asks me when I'm coming back."

"And you tell her…"

"Still December….so far." He leaned back in his chair and studied her. "I just really wish I had some better options for Max. He must get bored, with only me to play with—and I have to work on my computer way too much."

"So if you had some good alternatives for Max…"

"I wouldn't think twice about staying if I knew it was the right thing for Max. I never knew Montana was so beautiful."

"Good." She grinned. "Then do I ever have a great alternative for you!"

SEVEN

"Isabelle?" Jack's heart lifted with sudden hope. "She's good with children?"

"The best. She was a teacher for over forty years, and they practically had to drag her out of the building when it was time for her to retire. The kids loved her. Now she does day care, and her waiting list is about a mile long. She's babysitting the kids and grandkids of some of her old students, even."

Just that fast, Jack felt his hopes plummet. "Then there's no way she'd have a place for Max—especially since he'd just be there occasionally."

"That's the key, though. I called her this morning, thinking you might need some extra help now and then. One of her part-time kids has moved away, and she'll let you take that spot if you want it. When you leave, she'll fill it with a more permanent arrangement."

"That's unbelievable. Max will have a chance to

play with other kids, and he won't have to be so bored while I'm working. Thanks!"

"No problem. I think it helps everyone, really. She's got a boy just about his age who would love to have a playmate."

Jack wanted to do more than say thanks. He wanted to give her a hug, and then kiss her for good measure. But this was a business relationship, nothing more.

Landlord.

Boarder.

And if he let that line blur, he knew he'd regret it when it came time to leave town. Her life was here, and his was almost fifteen hundred miles away. And how did you move on and leave someone like her behind?

When some customers walked into the store, Erin went over to the cash register. Jack glanced at his watch and winced.

"Hey, buddy, time to go home," he murmured. He lifted the sleepy child into his arms, dropped a ten on the table and took him to the house next door.

With luck the boy would go back to sleep and give Jack some much needed time on the computer.

But as soon as they stepped in the door, Max came fully awake. "Can we go see the pony again?" he asked, wriggling out of Jack's arms to the floor.

Jack laughed. "Another time, sport. I think she's pretty tired. Anyway, it'll be suppertime before long."

"What about Charlie? Can I go play with him?"

"I think he's taking a nap. And Erin looks pretty busy right now."

"What about Go Fish?"

It was a game the child loved, but it could go on and on and on. "Maybe a little later if you find all the cards and put them on the table."

There would now be an occasional reprieve, but the weight of parenting still settled heavily on Jack's shoulders. He'd teased Janie, asking how one small child could so fully occupy her days. And now he knew.

Max was a full-time job if a guy did it right. If he made sure the child was clean and fed and entertained and read to and bathed, and properly put to bed at night. No wonder Janie hadn't gone back into real estate full-time after Max was born. So how did single mothers manage year after year?

The thought exhausted him.

And it made him wish for one last day with his sister, so he could tell her how proud he was of her…and how he'd do his best to raise her son.

After four rounds of Go Fish, a long bath and the usual nightly snack of an apple and string cheese, Max finally went to sleep. The next three or four hours stretching out before Jack were filled with possibilities—all of which had to involve staying at home. With a sigh he walked into the spare bedroom and fired up his laptop, then got to work. But instead of focusing on the stock market and client portfolios, he found his thoughts kept turning back to Erin.

And the kiss he hadn't taken.

The following week brought cold and rain, dark, threatening skies that turned the brilliant, emerging fall colors into a monochrome panorama in shades of gray.

The weather did give Erin lots of time to clean and organize and polish the little general store until it sparkled.

The downside was that there'd been so much time to do just that—because business was so slow.

She'd even seen less of Jack and Max, because Isabelle had agreed to watch Max several days this week while Jack caught up on his office work.

Her one steady customer proved to be the least likely of all: Ollie, who had developed a fondness for her sweet rolls and who turned up at eight o'clock every morning on his own, his crumpled cowboy hat in his hands and his wide face wreathed in a beatific smile.

Each day he pulled a double handful of pennies, nickels and dimes from his bulging jacket pockets and dumped them on the counter, then laboriously pushed them into tipsy stacks until he had enough for two rolls and a coffee.

Watching him touched her more deeply each day. He could've asked for a handout, and she would've given him one. She'd even *offered* one day, but he'd proudly shaken his head while continuing to count those piles of coins.

By Friday his pockets were nearly empty, and on Saturday he looked forlornly through the front window without stepping inside. And that nearly broke her heart.

Why weren't people helping him more?

Yet, she was just as guilty. How many times had she dropped money in a collection plate for some cause without ever taking action herself?

"So what do you think, Charlie?" Erin mused aloud. "Do we need some help around here? Can we even afford it?"

Curled up on his bed behind the cash register, Charlie looked up at her, his eyebrows wiggling up and down and his tail thumping against the wall.

"I'll take that as a yes." She went to the front door and opened it to a gust of damp wind. An eddy of dry leaves blew in and skittered across the floor. "Aren't you coming inside?" she called out. "It's kind of chilly out here."

Ollie's shoulders drooped and he started to shuffle away.

"Wait, come back. I need to ask you something."

He stopped and turned back with a hunted expression in his eyes. "Got no money."

"I need some help, and I thought you might like

the job. It's just some sweeping, but you could earn money to take home."

"Enough for rolls?"

"More than that. Say, ten dollars an hour and just a couple hours a day? But when the snow comes, you could earn more by shoveling."

He beamed. "I watch out for you, too."

"No, just some sweeping, and maybe some odd jobs here and there."

"Take care of you, too."

An image of the hulking man-child as her constant bodyguard in this small town made her smile. "Just the sweeping, really."

"No." He lifted his chin to a stubborn angle. "I watch out for you 'cause of the bad man."

A chill snaked across her skin. "What bad man? Who?"

"The one who comes and watches you sleep."

EIGHT

Erin didn't recognize the deputy who arrived an hour later in an unmarked car, straight from manning a speed trap he'd set up on County Road 33.

Apparently he'd been successful and wanted more of the action, because he'd been fidgeting and checking his watch since climbing from behind the wheel.

He glanced down at his clipboard, then tramped around the exterior of the cottage once again. "I don't see anything obvious. No unusual litter, no places worn down in the grass where someone has been taking a regular position outside your windows. So you say this guy comes at night and watches you through the windows?"

"That's what Ollie said. I haven't seen anything myself."

"Ollie. Where is he again?"

"He took off as soon as he saw your uniform. He's a little shy."

"So you've got a window peeper you haven't seen and a witness who has disappeared." The deputy cleared his throat. "You do realize that Ollie Mattson probably isn't a very dependable source of information."

"I know he has some mental challenges, but he sure seemed convinced about what he'd seen."

"We've also got a report from about ten days ago, when you thought there was an intruder in your store."

Erin sighed. "And I didn't see that guy, either. I heard him, but he slipped away. I know this all sounds crazy."

"Do you know of anyone who would want to harass you? An angry ex-boyfriend or husband, maybe?"

"I haven't had a relationship with anyone who might be volatile. Just some nice guys I dated one at a time. No one who would be jealous or possessive. In fact, all three of them are now happily married and live in Denver."

"What about business rivals or difficult customers? Any altercations over the last few months? Testy neighbors or relatives?"

"Nope." She bit her lower lip. "There was the Laura Warner murder years back. She was my cousin. But five years ago the guy who killed her turned up dead himself, according to the sheriff."

"Ahh." The deputy eyed her with compassion.

"You took over this store for your grandfather, didn't you? Not long ago?"

"That's right."

"It's got to be tough, coming back with all those memories. I've heard about the Warner case, but it was before my time." The radio in his patrol car crackled, and he canted his head to decipher a static-filled message. "I need to go, but I'll file this report so there's a record of your call in case anything else happens."

She nodded.

"Be sure to lock your windows and doors, and leave a light on when you leave the place at night. You might want to look into installing more security lights on the property, too. The one in front of the store doesn't cover the back door, but a new one in back would also cover the cottage pretty well."

"I'll make some calls today. I also intend to get a security system. I just haven't had a chance to look into it yet."

"What about caller ID?"

"I just bought one and hooked it up. And I took another step—a big guard dog." She gave the deputy a rueful smile and tipped her head toward Charlie, who had flopped at her side to rest his head on her shoe. The dog hadn't stopped wagging its tail since the deputy appeared. "But as you can see, he hasn't grown into his consistent protective mode quite yet. He does let me know about interlopers—as long as they're chipmunks and squirrels."

The deputy looked at Charlie and chuckled. "I was just going to suggest that you keep your dog in your bedroom at night, but I'm not sure he'd be much help."

"Charlie's working on it. He's still a baby."

She watched the deputy drive away, feeling only frustration, instead of relief.

He'd been polite. He'd taken time to look for possible clues. But he was right. Maybe Ollie *hadn't* really seen someone from a distance. And maybe everything else had just been her imagination, born of her fears over a long ago tragedy.

From inside the store came the ring of the telephone.

Grow up, she admonished herself as she turned to go back inside. *And have faith.*

But no one responded when she picked up the phone. All she heard was the sound of rapid breathing.

"Hello?" she said again, glancing at the caller ID. *Not available.* "Who is this?"

"The cop didn't find anything, did he," a man said flatly. "I suppose that makes you wonder if you're just imagining things. And now," he added with harsh laugh, "the cops won't be so quick to respond to someone who keeps crying wolf. Too bad…for you."

He hung up with a soft, deliberate click that sent a chill through her veins.

The caller *knew* the deputy had stopped by.

Someone with a police scanner could've heard that a patrol car had been dispatched to her address, but to hear the call they'd need to be within range of this 911 district. Which meant the caller had to be close.

Or maybe he was even closer—and standing in the shadows. Maybe he'd *seen* the deputy shake his head and drive away.

Was he watching the store through his binoculars even now? And *why?*

She certainly didn't have much to steal—and certainly nothing worth the risk of capture and incarceration. She had an old digital camera and an even older laptop. She didn't own a fancy computer or giant, flat-screen TV or have jewels stashed in her bureau. There wasn't a high-end sound system in her cottage. Her car was nine years old and didn't even have GPS; she didn't own original artwork or anything else of much interest.

And heaven knew there wasn't much in the store's cash register or in her bank account.

She stared out the windows of the cozy little store that had offered such warmth and fascination when she was a child. It had always been a place of laughter and her grandparents' loving devotion.

But now, she only felt the chill and desolation of

the approaching early snow that had been predicted for tonight.

And it was a long time before she remembered to put the phone receiver down.

Saturday dawned bright and sunny, turning the light dusting of snow into a landscape of sparkling sequins and lifting Erin's spirits. The heavier, predicted snowfall had missed them, and by afternoon, the thermometer had hit forty degrees.

She eyed a poster pinned to the bulletin board at the front of the store. "I wonder if it's too late to sign up," she mused under her breath.

At her shoulder an old man who'd come in to buy bread squinted at the sign. "That's the church potluck and bazaar. Don't need no signing up. Just go tonight. Me and the missus always do. She brings her famous peach pie every year."

"Sounds delicious."

"And you, young lady, could bring those good rolls of yours. They'd be a hit." He rubbed his jaw, thinking. "Might even help spread the word and bring in a lot more customers to your store."

She grinned. "An even better reason to attend."

He touched the brim of his old-fashioned fedora. "It was slow during the winters for Pete, too. Don't worry none about that. Tell that renter of yours to come along. People come from all over the county and have a great time. Kids, too. They have games and such for the little ones."

After the man left, Erin turned to the phone by the cash register and dialed Jack's number. "Hey, have I got some exciting plans for you!"

"Exciting plans, huh?" Jack teased, eyeing the crowd of people in the parking lot of Lost Falls Community Church. "I don't think we're going to make it into the church until Tuesday."

"Take a look at Max."

Eyes wide, the child was staring at the group of kids playing tag on the perimeter of the crowd waiting to enter a side door leading into the church basement. At just five he wasn't quite brave enough to join them, but she could see the longing in his eyes.

"I checked on Sunday-school times for this weekend. He'd enjoy going while we're still here, don't you think? He'd get to be with more kids his own age."

"I'm sure he'd like that, and it's sure important to help kids develop their faith at an early age." She felt a flash of melancholy at the reminder of how soon they'd be leaving Montana. "You've got plenty of time to give him the opportunity."

They moved toward the crowd and her hand brushed Jack's, sending a little shiver up her arm. He looked down at her and smiled, and she wondered if he'd felt the same sensation.

Maybe so, because a moment later he threaded his fingers through hers. "It's a beautiful night, isn't it? Just look at those stars."

Max looked up, too. "Millions and *millions*."

"That's because it's so dark up here. I'm in awe every time I see them at this altitude and so far from city lights. It's like you could almost reach up and catch them in your hand."

They drew closer to the crowd and Jack gave her hand an extra squeeze, then let go and lifted Max up in his arms. "What do you think, buddy?"

"I'm *hungry.*"

More people had come up behind them, and laughter rippled through those nearby.

"Just like a child—most important things first."

At the familiar voice, Erin turned and saw Martha, the postmistress, with her husband. And beyond them, a number of familiar faces—locals who had started coming to the store in slowly increasing numbers to chat over coffee by the potbellied stove or to buy their staples for the week.

"Have you heard from your grandfather? I miss him stopping in the post office every afternoon."

"Just a postcard this week. I've called him a few times, but he must be having way too much fun. He still hasn't called me back."

Martha laughed. "He's been talking about Florida for so long that I bet he can't believe he's finally there."

Erin suddenly felt as though she was being watched, and she glanced over her shoulder. "He should have gone a long time ago so he could enjoy it even more."

"He never felt right about selling your grandmother's store. She loved it so—it was the center of the community, and she must have made friends with every last person in the county." Martha's husband touched her arm and nodded toward some people standing nearby. "Excuse us—we're going to join our daughter and her family. See you inside."

Jack and Max had moved forward with the rest of the crowd. Erin started toward them—but again, felt that uneasy sensation at the back of her neck, though she could see nothing unusual when she looked around.

Someone brushed past her and knocked her arm. She stumbled half a step forward. Her purse fell at her feet.

"'Scuse me," a low, vaguely familiar male voice growled.

He smelled of sweat and cigarettes, and she fought the urge to recoil. "No problem."

She swiftly bent to pick up her purse. Her fingertips collided with a rough, hairy male hand closing over the handle. "Hey!"

He jerked hard, but she held tight and twisted away. Wedging herself between him and his quarry, she delivered a hard backward blow with her elbow that sank into his belly.

With a grunt and a low curse, he melted into the darkness, leaving her stunned and breathless, her heart racing.

She spun around, searching, but the security lights were closer to the church, and out here the dim wash of light and deep, dark shadows hid both his attempt at theft and his escape from the scattering of people this far away. Distracted by conversation and laughter, no one was even looking her way.

The voice. Where had she heard it?

And had someone actually tried to steal her purse, in the middle of the church parking lot?

NINE

"You look pale as chalk," Jack said when Erin finally caught up with him at the church door. He led her to one side, away from the others standing in line. Then he put Max down and took her shoulders in his hands to search her face. "Are you ill? Is something wrong?"

"I fell behind, and someone tried to grab my purse. I'm sure of it." She rubbed her right wrist. "I held on and elbowed him pretty hard. Why me, out of all these people?"

Jack's dark eyebrows drew together in concern. "Where is he? Did anyone catch him?"

"I don't think anyone else even saw him, he was gone so fast. I asked a few people, but no one else noticed what happened." She saw the questions in Jack's eyes. "And no, he didn't just inadvertently blunder into me. He jostled me, then tried to grab the strap. He swore when he couldn't wrench it away from me."

"Do you want to call the sheriff?"

"I didn't see the guy's face, so I couldn't identify him. And he didn't take anything."

"Still, you could've been hurt, Erin. I don't like this at all."

"I'd sure like to know if he's the same guy Ollie has seen outside my window."

Jack frowned. "One *could* ask what Ollie was doing out late at night, prowling around so he'd be there to see that happen. Maybe *he's* the one who has been doing it."

Erin thought for a moment, then shook her head. "I doubt that. He doesn't say much. But you just have to look in his eyes to see there's no guile there whatsoever. I think he must be one of those completely open and honest people, and that's just so rare."

"But maybe he could be convinced to do something—or even be coerced. Maybe he wouldn't think to question what he was told to do."

"I don't believe it's possible. Not since I've gotten to know him better. But Barry…that's a different story. I wonder if he smokes."

Max tugged at the sleeve of Jack's denim jacket. "Can we eat now? I'm hungry."

A subtle, deeper emotion darkened Jack's eyes, and for a moment she thought he was going to draw her into his arms. And in that moment she hoped he would—even with all the people nearby.

But then he dropped his hands from her shoulders, swung Max up onto his shoulders and reached for her hand. "I think we'd better get back in line before this poor little boy starves, don't you? But this time let's stick together."

The posters around town had advertised a potluck dinner, some sort of musical entertainment and a bazaar with a silent auction as its big draw. A perfect night for making his next move.

Erin Cole and everyone else in this Podunk town seemed to be at the church right now. Even that renter of hers and his kid were there—and finding a time with *them* out of the way had been nearly impossible.

The keys were a minor inconvenience.

He'd nabbed a big set the first time he'd broken into the general store, but then he hadn't been able to move quick enough and she'd had time to change the most important locks. Tonight she'd stubbornly held on to her purse, and he hadn't dared make a scene with so many people within shouting distance.

But even without keys, entering her cottage had been a breeze. One of the old windows was unlocked and rose easily with the twist of a crowbar. A sharp kick and a few choice words sent her stupid dog cowering behind the sofa.

And now he had the place to himself.

Glancing at his watch, he mentally scheduled his

time. Twenty minutes in the bedroom. Twenty each in the living room and kitchen. An hour in the closets—and he'd start with them as they were the most likely location for what he was after. If he was careful, methodical, she'd never even know he'd been inside.

Though by now the cops probably thought she was a crackpot and wouldn't give her calls a second thought—especially if there was no damage and no missing property other than a small, very special item that might have been easily misplaced, anyway.

In the bedroom he considered the jewelry box on the dresser, then discounted it as too small to hold what he was after. The cash next to it beckoned to him, but he left it alone and smiled. He could see it now.

She would walk through this cramped place.

Sense something was different.

Maybe she'd notice an object was slightly out of place, and her fear would start to build. But then she—and the cops, if she foolishly called them again—would notice the untouched money and jewelry and realize that a so-called break-in never could have occurred. And if he found what he was after, even that missing object wouldn't concern them because they wouldn't believe she hadn't mislaid it.

He laughed aloud. They might even assume that she'd lied about its loss just to make an insurance claim.

He smiled to himself, feeling a surge of power as

he readjusted his latex gloves. It didn't take brute strength to circumvent the law. It took cunning. Superior intellect. And very careful planning.

And now he had the whole evening to finally retrieve the one thing that stood between him and a life sentence for the unfortunate incident last month.

If Erin showed up a little too soon, it would be her own, very unfortunate mistake. And if she wasn't careful, it might be the last one she'd ever make.

After two hours he'd methodically removed, examined and replaced the contents of the closets, checked all the shelves and searched the bureau drawers. *Nothing.*

The clock was ticking.

The whining dog was driving him mad.

And both were making it hard to listen for any sound of someone approaching outside. He still had places left to search. And then he heard it—exactly what he'd feared.

A twig snapped.

Then another.

Voices. Erin's and a deep male voice, followed by soft laughter. What was she doing back so soon?

He felt for the comforting weight of the .38 snubbie in his jacket pocket and froze, judging the distance to the front door. No way he could make it out the door in time without being seen. The kitchen door on the side of the cottage was in view of the path, too, and wasn't an option, either.

Which meant trying to crawl out through one of the narrow back windows, or staying and permanently eliminating anyone who might prove to be a complication.

The jacketed hollow points in the revolver would stop anyone coming in the door. But taking two of them down left way too much chance for error, all the shoot-'em-up cop-show fairy-tale dramatics notwithstanding.

A key scraped into the dead bolt. Turned with a soft screech.

He glanced around to make sure nothing had been disturbed, then doused his pencil-thin flashlight.

He raced for the bedroom and stripped off his jacket, dropped it out of the open window, then started to wedge himself feet first through the tight opening.

From the living room came the sound of the front door squeaking open, then closing.

Panicking now, he wriggled harder—and then he noticed something white and slim under the bed, gleaming in a faint beam of moonlight. *Yes.*

He pedaled against the outside of the cottage to scramble back inside. Grabbed his prize, then dove for the window, his heart pounding, and shoved himself through.

He gently eased the window sash closed, picked

up his jacket and flattened himself against the cottage until he heard the sound of a car driving away and saw the bathroom light come on, its glow reflecting off the snow.

He had her laptop.

He needed one other thing, but at least it would be a good start. Or should he just go back in and get this over with?

He could promise he wouldn't hurt her. Force her to give him what he needed and then eliminate her, once and for all. This whole nightmare could be done with just that fast.

The temptation burned in his gut and he took a step back toward the window, flexing his fists. But small-town murders were messy affairs. He already had one on his hands, and where had it gotten him?

Nope, this time he would do everything right. And then he could finally live the life he so richly deserved.

Ollie appeared at the back door of the store the next morning at six o'clock, just as Erin was putting the first batch of caramel rolls into the oven.

Fat, lazy flakes of snow swirled about him like confetti, adding to the blanket of white on his hat and shoulders. "I can shovel," he said. "Okay?"

"Do you need to come in and warm up first? That coat doesn't look very warm."

He cast a longing look toward the warm, brightly

lit kitchen, but shook his head and stepped back out into the dusky morning, a rusted shovel in his hand.

"I'm just open from eight until three on Sundays," she called out the door. "But I'll be closed for about an hour, so I can go to church. Want to come with me?"

He shook his head so vigorously that she wondered what might have happened to him over the years. He'd apparently never gone to school, so he probably couldn't read. He was definitely shy. And he'd fled the moment he saw the deputy sheriff's cruiser pull up yesterday.

Had the locals taunted him through the years for being different? She didn't doubt it for a moment, and the thought of his lonely existence touched her heart.

By the time he came back in for his coffee and rolls, she was putting a second batch of rolls in the oven, and there were already eight customers huddled over their breakfasts in the café.

The bell over the front door jingled, and Jack walked in with Max. "Looks like we made it just in time for the last open table."

"There'll be a few people leaving before long." She bent down to smile at Max. "How do you like the snow?"

The little boy beamed. "A lot. We made snowballs!"

"Snowmen," Jack corrected. "Two, in the front yard. Though I hear the weather will be warming back up into Indian summer, so they'll soon be gone."

"We're going sledding after church!" Max announced.

Seeing the little boy smiling made her heart feel like it was two sizes too big for her chest. "That will be *lots* of fun."

"But we need a couple of sleds, if you have any," Jack added. "And since this may be Max's first and only snowfall up here, price is not an object."

"Believe me, this won't be your only snow if you stay until the beginning of December," Erin said dryly. "But I do have sleds. I saw some in the storage room just last night."

She took their order, and after delivering their food, she went out to the shed to bring in a collection of old-fashioned wooden sleds with metal runners, plastic saucers and a couple of toboggans that she arranged by the front door.

Max appeared at her elbow, his breakfast forgotten. "Wow," he breathed.

"So which one do you like best?"

"The long red one—with *sparkles*."

"Great choice. Does your uncle need one, too?"

Jack came over to study the options. "I'd take the toboggan if you'll come with us. What do you say?"

Surprised and a little flattered, she hesitated, then shook her head. "I should probably stay here and tend to the store. But it's nice of you to ask."

"This is a big sale," he said with a smile. "You'd

have to sell an awful lot of coffee to match it. And just think of the company—two Texans who don't know a thing about sledding. You'll have a good laugh, if nothing else."

"Please?" Max danced from one foot to the other, his eyes gleaming.

"We owe you a social invitation after last night at the church. We had a good time, didn't we, Max?"

The boy nodded and she wavered. It *had* been a wonderful evening, with a wonderful meal, several hours of conversation and then a musical comedy by the church youth group. How many people would come by the store during the few hours she'd be out, anyway?

And then you'll have more time with Jack, a small voice whispered in her heart. *It won't be long and he'll be gone.*

She nodded a little reluctantly. "I do know some good hills near here. Nice and long, not too steep. If you want, I'll bring a thermos of hot chocolate. It'll help keep everyone warm."

"Sounds like something right out of a Norman Rockwell painting." Jack flashed a smile that deepened the dimples bracketing his mouth and sent tingles of awareness straight to her heart. "We'll be dreaming about it long after we go south."

"I'll do you one better. I'll bring my camera and take lots of shots. And then Max can prove to his friends back home that he played in our good Montana powder."

Jack glanced at his watch. "If it works for you we'll be back at three. Be ready for the time of your life on those rugged Montana mountains!"

She'd dated a number of nice guys who had treated her well. Pleasant, educated and—thankfully—employed, all of them might have been good, solid husband material, but none had ever made her feel a little zing of excitement with just a touch of his hand.

But Jack had, and he hadn't even been trying. What would it be like to be held in his arms and to kiss him properly—with all the passion and deep emotion of a real relationship?

She'd never know. Their paths had been set on different courses long before they'd ever met, and even now the end was in sight. But today they'd have fun. The three of them, all playing with the joyous abandon of children.

And though her photographs would be meant as gifts for little Max, they would also be a gift for herself. A treasured memory, from the time when a complete stranger had walked into her life and touched her heart.

Jack and Max appeared at the front door of her cottage at three, just as promised. Max waddled in, bundled up in a second coat, a scarf and two pairs of mittens, and Erin could barely hold back her smile.

Jack was incredibly handsome in a trim-fitting black ski jacket and red turtleneck that accented his dark hair and eyes. Max looked as roly-poly as the kid brother in her favorite Christmas movie about a quest for a BB gun from Santa.

"It's…um…not that cold, believe it or not."

Jack hovered over the boy. "But all that snow…"

"People ski up here in light jackets on days like this." He still looked concerned, and that *did* make her smile. What was it that was so incredibly appealing about a man when he was so caring of a child? "But hey, bring it all, and you can judge when we get there. I just need to run out to my car to get my camera and snow boots from the trunk, and I'll be almost ready."

She dashed outside, retrieved the items and set them on the bench just inside her front door, then turned to the closet to reach for her ski jacket.

And for the second time that afternoon, she froze and stared at the contents of a closet.

The usual array of coats on hangers and boxes on the shelf seemed to be there. Everything was neatly stowed. Yet, hadn't the blue plastic container of gloves been stored on the left?

And didn't she always hang her leather coat way to the right, since she rarely wore it these days?

She'd felt an odd sense of premonition before opening her bedroom closet earlier today, too.

But nothing had been missing. Her jewelry box

and pair of ten-dollar bills on her dresser nearby hadn't been touched.

If there'd actually been an intruder, surely he would've nabbed anything of value within easy reach, wouldn't he?

Of course he would. She rolled her eyes. *Dearie, your imagination is running amok, and Jack will soon think you're crazy.*

Pulling on her jacket and boots, she dropped her digital camera into a pocket and turned to him with a smile. "I'm ready! And I just know this is going to be a wonderful day."

Winter in Montana was always breathtaking, with the soaring, snowy peaks rising against the sky and air so pure, so crystalline, that it nearly hurt to breathe.

But an early snow fall like this one, with the leaves still a blazing riot of color, was so beautiful it almost made her cry.

Heavy snow weighed down the fragile branches of the aspens with their bright yellow leaves, and blanketed the fierce oranges and reds of the hardwoods in a brilliant quilt of white with splashes of color blazing through. Farther up the mountainside, dense pine forests were of the deepest shades of green beneath a heavy frosting of white.

They drove over a sapphire stream, still gurgling freely on its way down from the mountains, the deep blue in stark contrast to the mounds of snow covering its banks.

Over the next rise, a panorama of steadily rising foothills stretched north and south to the horizon, and beyond them, the Rockies rose fierce and proud and massive.

"I've always thought that this was the most beautiful place on earth," Erin said softly as she stepped out of the car. "How could anyone stand here and deny the existence of God in the presence of such glorious scenery?"

Jack helped Max out of his car seat, then collected the sleds from the back of the SUV. He came to stand next to her as she looked out over the valley below and draped one arm around her shoulders.

He was silent for a long time, and then he grinned and looked down at her. "That is so true. Thank you for bringing us here. This is unbelievable."

"Are we going down that big hill?" Max asked, his voice filled with awe.

Erin laughed. "Nope. Look behind you. The hills are a lot more gentle going the other way, but they're nice and long."

The boy looked so darling in his puffy red jacket, bright blue snow pants and whimsical red-yellow-and-blue hat, that she reached for her camera and began snapping pictures.

When Jack started down one of the long hills with

Max on a sled, she jogged backward snapping pictures until she got bogged down in the deep powder and fell over.

Jack steered the sled into a tight turn to stop and ran over to offer her a hand. "Are you okay?"

Laughing, she lobbed a handful of the fluffy powder at him, though most of it fell back on her. "This snow is like tumbling into a vat of feathers. I'm just glad my camera has a waterproof housing or I'd be in big trouble."

He helped her up, then scooped her into his arms, carried her a few feet, and dropped her into a big drift. "I'm thinking that you already are."

Max ran over to join them, his cheeks rosy and his eyes sparkling, and Jack plopped him in the snow next to Erin.

"Can we stay here always? I like snow!"

"There's definitely a lot of it around here," Erin said. "This load will all melt, but when winter *really* hits, you'll be looking at a good hundred inches of snowpack. Believe it or not, we can have three hundred inches of actual snowfall."

Jack formed a loose snowball and tossed it out over the valley, then offered her another hand up, his eyes twinkling. "Trust me?"

She hesitated, then laughed and took his hand. This time, he helped her up and dusted the snow from her jacket.

"Do you guys ever get snow in Texas?"

"Not often. When we do, everyone hurries out to take pictures—but it's nothing compared to this."

She felt a tug at her heart, thinking about them going back to Texas. "So maybe you'll come back again next winter to play in the snow?"

It was silly to ask. He could find snow a lot closer than way up here in Montana, and every problem that had led Jack here now would surely be resolved by then.

Jack's company problems would be straightened out. He and Max would have bonded well by then, and the boy would need to be in school full-time, not gallivanting in the mountains for months.

All would be well for them—but she'd probably never see either of them again.

"Okay, you two—let's get serious about sledding before we all get too cold!" She snapped several photos of Max playing in the drift, then some of Jack and Max together, their cheeks rosy from the cold, against a background of snow-frosted pines and an ice-blue sky.

One perfect shot after another, and she greedily took them all, wanting to preserve every moment of this perfect day. But a few shots later the camera's screen read Card Full.

She stared at it in disbelief. "Noooo!"

Jack came to stand behind her and peered over her shoulder. "It quit working?"

"How can a four-gig memory card be full? I thought I'd changed it." She groaned, remembering the last time she'd used it. "But I guess not. I've got my friend Linda's entire wedding on it, plus a lot of candid shots of the guests and the pretty setting."

He playfully gave her shoulder a squeeze. "So now it looks like you'll just have to have fun with us, instead. C'mon—put the camera away and let's go."

"You're right." She dropped the camera into an inside zippered pocket of her coat and grinned at Max. "Last one to the sled has to sit in the back!"

The little boy took off running, floundered in the snow, and bounded off again. Laughing, she started after him at a walk, but Jack touched her arm and she turned back. "What?"

"Thanks for all of this. I never thought I'd see Max so happy again. You've been such a blessing for him." He looked down at her, his beautiful, dark eyes intense, then he reached up to frame her face with his hands and brushed a kiss over her mouth. "Max will never forget this day…and neither will I."

TEN

The temperature dropped as the sun slipped behind the mountains and brilliant streaks of rose and lavender and gold filled the western sky.

The day was over and it was time to get home before the narrow, snowy mountain road was too difficult to navigate in the dark.

"I wish the day didn't have to end," Erin said with a rueful smile. "Any chance you guys would like sloppy joes and cocoa at my place?"

Jack glanced in the rearview mirror. "From the looks of it, Max is nearly asleep. I'd better get him home. But you're welcome to come over. He's bound to wake up in an hour or two, and we could have supper at my place, instead. Say, maybe seven?"

"Perfect. I'll bring my laptop and camera's memory card, so you two can see the pictures I took today. If you like any of them, I can have prints made."

"I'd appreciate that. The only problem is that there aren't any of you."

She grinned. *"That's* the benefit of being on the other side of the camera."

"Max will want to remember everything about this trip, though. It wasn't until Janie died that I realized just how important lots of photographs are. Sometimes you just can't go back and take what you missed, and she was the one who documented all the special events in our family, too."

In the deepening twilight, the glow of the dash-board lights illuminated the lines and planes of his rugged face, the shadows throwing his high cheek-bones and strong jaw into sharp relief. The pain of losing his sister showed in the grim lines of his mouth.

"You must miss her terribly. I'm so sorry about your loss."

"It's Max who has the greatest burden. A child's mother is the center of his universe, and losing both her and his dad was devastating. He was hysterical at first, then he simply withdrew—as if his emotions were just...gone. The counselor said it happened because he couldn't deal with the pain."

"That sure doesn't seem surprising when you say it like that."

His expression darkened. "Things might have been a little easier, but then my fiancée walked out— she said she just couldn't cope with all the drama or with the prospect of being an instant mom for a five-year-old."

Erin snorted indignantly. "How shallow was that? She didn't deserve either one of you."

"Maybe, but the breakup happened at a very bad time—when Max could've used her love and attention." He gave a short laugh. "I already knew that if something was an inconvenience, she didn't bother, but until Janie's death everything else had been *minor.*"

He drove in silence, taking several tight turns with his full attention on the snow-packed highway, then settled back and relaxed behind the wheel when the terrain opened up into a small meadow on the edge of Lost Falls. "After that fiasco, it'll be a long time before I'm ready to try anything serious again. How about you?"

"I was close a couple times, but it just never seemed right. The first time, we were awfully young, too young for that kind of commitment. A person can change so much in their early twenties." She smiled and gave a little shrug. "And sometimes not enough. And later, another boyfriend and I realized that we were settling for 'available' and not 'soul mate,' and that has definitely dimmed my enthusiasm for trying again. I'd rather just have my independence."

He cut a glance at her, the laugh lines at the corners of his eyes deepening. "Dimmed enthusiasm. That makes your future prospects sound sort of grim."

"Think about it. You date someone for what—six months, a year, maybe two? And you think you know them. Or worse, some people even live together, thinking it's a true test. But it isn't, because everyone is still on their best behavior, knowing they could lose out if they aren't careful." She took a deep breath. "But then you get married and the masks come off. And what then?"

"Happily-ever-after wedded bliss?" Jack winked at her. "My mother assures me that it's so."

"She sounds like a sweet lady."

"And one who wants to see me married off so Max will have a stable home…and she'll have the prospect of more grandkids. But I'm afraid she's out of luck."

Erin laughed. "We are quite the jaded pair."

"Realistic."

"And that, too." They were approaching the turn-off for Millie's, and Erin motioned him to turn in right in front of the store. "You can just drop me off here. I'll walk around back and let Charlie out for a while, and then I'll come over."

He frowned. "It's awfully dark back there. I'll go with you."

"And leave Max alone in the car? No need." She opened up the door and hopped out. "See you in an hour or so."

Still, he backed up a few yards and made a three-point turn so his headlights flooded the front of the cottage out back, and waited until she got inside. Only when she'd flipped on a number of interior lights did she see his headlights swing away.

Charlie whined anxiously from his wire kennel in the laundry room, so she took him out first and let him loose in the fenced yard. He raced around the perimeter, barking furiously, as if determined to chase any interlopers away, then he disappeared and fell silent—probably after finding one of his giant rawhide chew toys.

She waited for a minute, then shrugged and went inside to draw a hot bath laced with her favorite lavender-and-lily bath oil.

As she sank into the fragrant water, she leaned back and closed her eyes, feeling her cold muscles relax in the delicious heat until she felt as boneless as a rag doll.

What a lovely day. What a perfectly lovely day...

Drifting and dreaming, she floated on powdery snow in a sunlit field...then a discordant note jarred her thoughts. Something was whining. Clawing at a door. Charlie?

Startled, she jerked awake and shivered in the now cool bathwater. She grabbed the watch she'd laid at the edge of the tub. *Seven?* It couldn't be seven.

Launching herself out of the tub, she quickly dried off and hunted through her closet, then settled on a pair of black slacks and a bulky-knit crimson sweater before going to the back door. Sure enough, Charlie was sorrowfully staring through the glass, his paws planted halfway up the door.

"I am so, so sorry," she said as she let him inside and relocked the dead bolt.

Instead of giving her his usual, exuberant welcome, or going to his dog bowls to demand food and water, he hung his head and went back inside his kennel, where he plopped down with his head facing out and resting it on his paws.

"Are you sulking?"

He didn't stir.

"I suppose you would've liked sledding today."

His tail thumped once against the side of the kennel.

"And…I suppose you think I forgot you outside. Which I did."

Again, a single, halfhearted thump.

"Maybe you could come with me tonight. Max would like that, and you've been alone a lot today. I just need to get my camera and laptop, and we can pick up a few groceries in the store. Okay?"

She went into the bedroom and crouched to reach under the bed, then rocked back on her heels. Where was it? Swiveling, she glanced around the room. It was always under the bed, out of sight, unless she was using it here or at the shop. *Always.*

After a thorough search of every possible place, she picked up her camera, whistled to Charlie and went to the store. There she hunted through the store with him close at her heels, while grabbing the ingredients for supper along the way.

The laptop wasn't in the store, either.

She stared at her reflection in the front windows of the store, suddenly uneasy. She couldn't see out, but anyone could see in, as clearly as if she was on TV. What if someone was out there watching her every move?

She'd had that odd feeling when pulling her jacket from the closet. A sense that things weren't exactly right. The same sensation in the bedroom. Yet nothing had appeared to be missing until now. If someone had broken in to rob the place, why hadn't he snagged her jewelry box?

Her grandmother's pearls were inside. A considerable collection of Black Hills Gold she'd bought one piece at a time. The box, less than a foot long, would have been easy to carry, or its contents dumped into a pillowcase. And yet nothing inside was missing.

Which left the laptop as a specific target. But it was several years old and hardly a gem in today's rapidly changing technology market.

So who would want it...and why?

"I hope you don't mind Charlie coming along," Erin said as Jack ushered her into his kitchen. "He's been alone all day, and he seems depressed."

Jack reached down to ruffle the fur behind the dog's ears. "No problem. Max loves him."

"Lie down, Charlie." She watched the pup obediently go to the corner by the kitchen table and plop down, then look around. "It's so quiet here. Where's Max?"

"Still sleeping, but last time I looked he was starting to stir." He unpacked the grocery sack while she slipped out of her jacket.

"Sorry I'm late." She blew at her bangs. "I fell asleep in the bathtub, had to take Charlie outside, needed to pick these groceries and—unfortunately—spent a lot of time searching for my laptop."

"Where'd you find it?"

"I didn't. I usually stow it in a computer bag under the bed when I leave, so it isn't too tempting to someone breaking in." She sighed in frustration. "I searched the cottage, top to bottom. Then I looked around the store, just in case."

"Did someone take it?"

"I think so, but that's what's strange. I had jewelry in plain sight on the bureau, along with some cash, and those things weren't touched. Why would someone want an old laptop and not nab the twenty dollars?"

"I lost my laptop in my house once. It was lying on the carpet and got nudged under a sofa. Another time, I found it on an end table under a pile of newspapers."

"Well, I looked everywhere twice, and mine is

gone. But when I call this in, the sheriff is going to think I'm just imagining things again. What proof do I have that it was ever here?" She bit her lower lip. "Even Isabelle thinks I'm worrying over nothing, yet more and more things keep happening. If only I'd had a recording of the phone call, it would be *something* to go on."

Jack turned sharply to look at her. "You got a phone call?"

"A heavy breather at first…then he mocked my inability to prove I'd had any trouble whatsoever." She opened the cupboard and pulled out a frying pan, turned on the stove and the oven, then dumped a package of ground beef into the pan. "I know he was trying to scare me, but he was right. No proof. And of course, the caller ID said the number was unavailable."

"You need a security system."

"*And* a security light or two behind the store. I've already called the power company, but they can't get at the light for another week or two." She opened several drawers until she found a plastic spatula, then started breaking up the browning ground beef. "Want to stir up that box of brownies?"

He nodded, checked the box and retrieved three eggs from the fridge, then washed his hands at the sink. "What about the security system?"

"A guy is coming up from Red Lodge on Wednesday." She watched him neatly crack each egg one-handed and grinned. "Hey, you're pretty good."

"College job at an all-night diner. Just the basics." He tossed the shells in the trash. "Frankly I'm worried about you staying alone at that cottage, if Ollie really saw someone lurking by your windows at night. You've had a threatening phone call and now your laptop is missing. Whoever this guy is, he's escalating."

"But if he's actually broken into the cottage, surely he saw that I have nothing of great value to steal. Don't those people usually go after fancy electronics and such?"

Jack pulled a bottle of canola oil from the cupboard and measured some into the bowl. "Maybe it's something else. Maybe…your grandfather was known for something. Coin collections. Or his aversion to banks, so he hid his cash in odd places."

She laughed at that. "Not Gramps. He's a firm believer in CDs and T-bills."

Max shuffled into the kitchen sleepy-eyed, but his face brightened when he saw Erin and the puppy. "You came!" he exclaimed, running over to the corner. He dropped to his knees and hugged Charlie's neck.

But instead of joyously licking the child's face and bounding into dizzying circles, the pup cringed and drew back.

"Look at that." She studied the cowering puppy,

and a sudden realization made her feel sick to her stomach. "He was in the cottage when we went to the church potluck dinner, and I left him loose when I got back because he's been doing well with his house-training. Ever since, he's been different—terrified, reclusive. I'll bet my intruder came while we were gone."

She called softly to Charlie. He whined, but when she called again, he belly-crawled across the floor to her. When she ran a hand over his body, he yelped when she touched his side.

Max's eyes widened. "Is he hurt?"

She gently examined his ribs. "There's no heat or swelling, but I'll bet he's bruised, right here." She looked up at Max. "Maybe a little, like when you fall down. I'll take him to the vet if he's still sore tomorrow."

"We've got Band-Aids."

"He's not bleeding, so I think we're okay." She smiled to reassure him. "Just don't pet his side, okay? Maybe it would be better if you just let him rest awhile." She stood, turned to Jack and lowered her voice. "I think he got kicked or hit, and I can't tell you how angry I feel. An old computer is one thing, but to hurt a sweet, trusting puppy is beyond comprehension."

"And now we know the guy is probably capable of violence." Jack nodded and briefly rested a hand at her cheek. "I'm worried about you, Erin."

"I'm a big girl. I won't do anything foolish."

"You need to call that sheriff. And now, I *definitely*

don't think you should be staying alone in that cottage until this guy is caught, or you have that security system in place. There's certainly room here—or maybe you could stay at the motel in town."

The options sounded appealing. But drawing danger to the rental house could risk the safety of a small child, and the old strip motel, set off in the pines and away from the lights of town, sounded even less secure.

"I've got a gun, actually. My grandfather's." She hoped her voice sounded more confident than she really felt. "So don't worry—I'll be just fine."

ELEVEN

After the supper dishes were done, Erin pulled her digital camera from the pocket of her coat. "If you have a computer handy, we can look at the sledding photos. Maybe I'll see a few that I can delete, and then I can get a shot of those two right now."

Max had finally lured Charlie from beneath the table, and the two of them were stretched out on the living-room floor. Max had one arm draped over the dog's shoulders and with the other hand he was turning the pages of *Go, Dog. Go!*

He was laboriously sounding out the words on each page, and if Erin didn't know better, she'd think the dog was actually looking at the storybook, too.

Jack brought out his laptop and opened it on the kitchen table, then turned it on. Once the startup process brought up the desktop, she slipped the card in and launched the photo program. A flood of photos rapidly populated the screen.

"Oh, my," she breathed. "I'd forgotten what a beautiful day it was for the wedding. It seems like a lifetime ago. I hadn't even looked at these until now."

Jack braced a hand on the table and leaned over her shoulder to peer at the tiny thumbnail views. "You should be a professional photographer."

"Thanks. I'd be nervous about taking that kind of responsibility, but I love taking candids for friends and relatives, then giving them an album for their first anniversary.

"This one was held in a state park close to Denver. It was just gorgeous, with the start of the fall colors and all those trees."

She clicked on the first photo and laughed when it filled the screen. "The bride, Linda, is one of my best friends, and the disgruntled flower girl is her niece. The ring bearer had just walloped her with his little satin pillow, so by the time I snapped the photo, both kids were in tears."

Jack chuckled. "Since your laptop is missing, go ahead and look through all of them while you have a chance. Max is busy, and I can check through the last package of mail my secretary forwarded up here."

She eagerly clicked on the next photo, then smiled up at him. "This is like opening birthday presents, getting to see how these all turned out."

Jack disappeared into one of the main-floor bedrooms, where he'd apparently set up an office, and she turned back to the photos.

A wave of nostalgia hit her as the wedding day unfolded before her eyes. Family. Friends. Joy and confidence shining in the couple's eyes. *I once thought I'd have that, too, Lord...but I guess that isn't what You have in store for me.*

She scrolled through several hundred shots, deleting the ones with obvious flaws, until she got to the departure of the bride and groom. Jack wasn't back yet and Max was still reading to the dog, so she continued into the several dozen or so that she'd taken of the surrounding park after Linda and her husband had left for their honeymoon.

"Breathtaking," she murmured, studying a glittery waterfall tumbling over rugged boulders. Aspens formed brilliant yellow sentinels framing the photo, their skeletal white trunks in stark contrast to the charcoal-gray rock.

Jack came out into the kitchen. "Did you say something?"

"If you have a minute, look at these with me. I used a 300mm telephoto to shoot these from across a river running through the park. Until now, I didn't know if they'd be sharp enough with that lens, but maybe they're okay."

She studied the photo a moment longer, then pressed Slide Show for the rest of the photos to move automatically from one to the next. "Maybe I could frame some prints and sell them in the store."

He nodded. "Or you could do a coffee-table book, though I have no idea of how one goes about getting those published. These are excellent shots."

"Well, oops. Guess I goofed on these."

She studied a series of photos with brilliantly backlit gold and ruby leaves that seemed to glow and leap from the screen. There was a stray male figure in each one, off to the side.

As the photos automatically marched past in slide-show mode, he appeared to be coming out of the undergrowth, then into full view, as if in a jerky, old-time movie.

"I was using motor drive to shoot these and didn't even notice him. I could try cropping him, but then the balance would be lost."

"You could try to use Photoshop to get him out."

"Or I could just add these to the wedding album—though come to think of it, he probably wasn't with us. I don't think there was a bridge anywhere in the area, so he couldn't have gotten over the river." She stopped the slide show and leaned forward, trying to make out his features, then hit Zoom to enlarge the view. "Yet we were in an awfully remote part of the park."

The sudden appearance of the man's surly features startled her. "What an unpleasant guy."

She increased the zoom until the photo turned grainy. Behind him was a long, dark shadow of something on the ground. A boulder? A log? If she let her imagination run wild, it could even be a pile of dirt from digging a good-size hole.

Jack frowned. "What is he holding—a rifle? I think it's a long handle of some kind. It's…it's…"

"Go back a frame or two."

They went through all the photos of the stranger, one by one, enlarging each. Watching the evolution of his dawning awareness that he was being photographed from afar. The morphing of his expression from smug to fierce.

Erin felt her heart beat faster. "I could be wrong, but it looks like a shovel to me. What was he doing in the middle of nowhere with something like that?"

"It *could* be a long walking stick. Lots of hikers carry them in the mountains. And I still think it could be the barrel of a rifle."

"Or a shovel," she repeated.

"If so, maybe he was illegally burying his dog out there to save the cost of cremation at a vet's. That could account for his expression at being caught on film."

"Or he could've been stealing protected vegetation of some kind," she suggested dryly.

"I know you're afraid that this might be something

far worse. Do you remember hearing anything on the news that night?"

She shook her head. "As soon as I finished taking these pictures, I hurried back to my car so I could head for Lost Falls. I had a long drive ahead of me, and I hate traveling late at night when I'm tired. I listened to CDs all the way."

"Maybe you should talk to your friends in Colorado and see if they remember anything."

"I will." She glanced at her watch. "It's still early enough. I think I'll run to the drugstore in Lost Falls and get prints made of these. You can send away for double prints or use their automatic machine. The store doesn't close until ten."

Max wandered over to the table. "Can I see the snow pictures now?"

"Of course you can, sweetheart." Erin gave him a quick hug and pulled him onto her lap. "Let's look at them right now, and then I'll get prints made for you, too."

Jack disappeared, then came back with an armload of their jackets. "We should go. I'll give you a ride, Erin."

"That's not necessary," she protested. "Really."

He tipped his head toward the windows and the black night beyond. He smiled, but there was a definite thread of steel in his voice. "Then let us come along just to make *me* feel better. Please."

* * *

Grace Millard had worked at the drugstore when Erin was a child, and she'd looked old and gray even then.

Now she appeared to be pushing 110, but she still had a spritely bounce to her step and a twinkle in her eye as she toddled over to the photo machine and gave it a swift, hard kick with a lace-up roper boot. "Silly thing. I swear it decides to balk like an old mule just to spite me. Try again."

Erin dutifully touched the proper buttons, but once again, all the lights flashed on and off, and then the screen read Service Needed.

"Humph." Grace folded her bony arms across her chest. "It was working earlier today for the Sampsons. They were in here for a good half hour printing their Hawaii pictures."

"How soon will a repairman be here to fix it?"

"He comes from Billings and has to put me on the schedule for when he's in the area. Could be a day, could be a week or two."

Jack glanced up at the clock. "Is there another place in town?"

"A couple of tourist shops have them, but those stores are closed till spring. Closest is Battle Creek. But that's thirty-six miles and the roads are pretty icy up that way. You'd never make it in time for tonight."

Erin sighed. "Not a good option."

"If it isn't a rush, you could just use the mailers. Cheaper, plus you get doubles and a CD copy, to boot. There's a pickup tomorrow and then they'd be back here in a week. Of course you get your memory cards back, empty and ready to go."

She could come back another day, but there'd still be no guarantee that the processing machine would be repaired. And keeping the memory card any longer sent an uneasy feeling twisting through her stomach.

She reached for one of the mailer envelopes, filled it out and sealed the memory card inside, then dropped it through the photo mailer slot in the counter.

She smiled at the older woman. "You sold me, Grace. Sounds like a good idea."

Grace tilted her head and gave her an odd look. "Is everything all right?"

"Fine—just busy."

Grace frowned. "Well, you just look mighty stressed. I think of you girls often, you know. I remember when you and your cousins would come to stay with Millie and Pete. You three were such scamps, and you all grew up to be such lovely young ladies." Grace shook her head sadly. "But poor little Laura… Oh, my. I'll never forget that night. Nosiree."

You and me both. Uncomfortable with the grisly memories that started creeping back into her thoughts, Erin hiked the strap of her purse higher on her shoulder and gave Jack a pointed look. "I guess we'd better get going, don't you think?"

They were just heading out the door when Grace called Erin's name. "I knew there was something I wanted to tell you, but I plumb forgot."

Erin stopped with one hand on the door and looked back with a smile. "What's that?"

"The nicest fella was here a while back, looking for you. Handsome as can be. He was asking all sorts of questions," Grace added in a conspiratorial voice. "Like he was real interested, if you know what I mean."

Erin stilled. "Did he give his name?"

Grace's snowy brows drew together as she thought. "Can't rightly say. I figured maybe he was an old beau of yours hoping to look you up."

"What did he look like?"

"Medium tall, nice face. Dark hair. Or maybe it was sort of sandy… Anyways, he was real proud to hear that you were running your grandpa's store and said he would look you up one of these days. Just thought you'd like to know."

By the time they reached the cottage, Max and Charlie were both asleep in the backseat.

Jack looked over his shoulder at them, then turned back to Erin. "I still don't like the idea of you staying here all alone. You heard that woman—some guy has been asking a lot of questions. Maybe he's the one causing all the trouble."

"I'll make sure every door and window is locked tight. I've got a cell phone and I've got Charlie. I'm not going to let anyone scare me out of my own home."

He hesitated, then opened his door and got out. "Come on, then. I'll go inside with you and check everything out."

"But, Max—"

"As soon as you step out of the car, I'll hit the locks. Max'll be fine for a couple minutes, and I'll only be a few yards away, at any rate."

She let Charlie out of the backseat and turned him loose in the yard, then unlocked the door of the cottage and reached inside to flip on the porch and interior lights.

Jack insisted on going inside first.

She watched from the doorway as he went from room to room and checked every closet, behind every door and under the bed, jiggling window locks and checking the back door as he went.

"All clear," he said on a long sigh, standing in the front doorway where he could keep an eye on his car and Max. "For now. Are you *sure* you won't change your mind and come with us?"

"I'm sure. I'll probably be up half the night, anyway, wading through invoices and such. I've got to regenerate a lot of bookkeeping for the store now that my laptop is gone."

He glanced at his watch. "I'll call you at ten o'clock just to check in. You've got my cell on your speed dial, right?"

She fought the urge to roll her eyes. "I will put it in. Promise."

"And you won't hesitate to call."

His eyes were warm and intense, searching hers as if he really, truly cared for her—as more than a landlord, a friend, an accidental neighbor. She felt a gentle sensation of warmth embrace her heart.

"Believe me, I'm not a high-maintenance woman. But yes, I'll call."

"Good." His gaze flicked toward the car, then back to her. "Because you're one of the most stubborn, independent women I've met, and it worries me. A lot."

"I can tell," she teased. "Now go home."

He started down the short flagstone walk, then pivoted and came back. Holding her with one arm around her shoulders and the other braced high on the door, he brushed a single kiss over her mouth, then rested his forehead against hers. "Keep safe."

And then he was gone.

TWELVE

Before settling down to work on the books for the store, Erin searched for the missing laptop once more, praying she'd missed it the first time.

She knew it would be wasted time. She'd searched every square inch of the place already. But finding it would mean that no one had broken into the cottage while she was at the church potluck. That no one had gone through her things.

Just the thought made her skin crawl.

But now, standing at the right angle, she could see shallow gouges in the sill of her bedroom window. She could imagine the tip of a crowbar working its way slowly, inexorably beneath the sash…and the window flying upward with a powerful jerk.

And then, staring into the twisted face of an intruder coiling to launch himself into the cottage…

She shook away the horrible images and snorted at her own foolishness. There'd been a theft. The guy had stolen the most valuable item in the cottage. So why would he bother to come back?

She strode through the cottage, checking the locks on the windows and doors once again, then sat cross-legged on her bed with Charlie at her side, thankful for his presence—even if he'd been sleeping and blissfully unaware of all possible dangers.

I guess he's the one who got it right, Lord. I just need to let go and have faith that You're here with me.

Her cell phone burst into its musical ringtone and she jumped, startled by the unexpected noise.

"Linda!" she managed, her voice shaking. "Good to hear your voice!"

"Oh, *no.*" A pause, then Linda continued, "I wasn't even thinking about the time. I just saw your message from earlier tonight and thought I'd return your call. I'm so sorry—I can call back at a decent hour."

"Please, don't hang up."

"Is something wrong?" Linda's voice grew cautious. Tentative. "Are you all right?"

What did Erin say to that? The truth would only worry an old friend who could do nothing to help from so far away, anyhow. "Tonight I was studying the photos I took at your wedding. What a beautiful day that was."

Linda chuckled. "That's why you called? Whew!"

"Well…not entirely. I took a lot of shots of the park itself, so you'd have those, too. But I inadvertently ended up with quite a few that show some guy down by the river."

Linda was silent.

"I know it sounds crazy, but I was using a tele-photo lens and hadn't even noticed he was in the pictures until now. But I think he must've seen me, because I caught him looking straight at the camera, and he looks absolutely livid."

"Can't you just delete the pictures?"

"Sure, but I've got this uneasy feeling that won't go away. He just looks…guilty, somehow. So I'm wondering if you remember anything about the local news that day. If anything bad happened in the area, for instance."

Another long silence.

"Linda?"

"I'm just thinking, but I guess I can't be much help. I left for the Caribbean with Carl on the afternoon of the wedding, and I wasn't paying attention to the news for *days* before that. So I don't have a clue. My advice? Delete those photos and forget about them."

"Well…maybe so."

"Or if you're still concerned, check the newspa-pers online. I'm pretty sure the local papers are archived." A male voice rumbled in the background. "Sorry—Carl says he needs the phone. But I'll call you back later, okay? Thanks a million for taking the pictures. I can't wait to see them!"

* * *

Ollie showed up in Millie's at eight in the morning and swept the store with painstaking care as always, then beamed down at her as he handed back the broom. "Good?"

"Very, *very* good. Thanks." She followed him into the café and served him his two caramel rolls and coffee. "I have something for you, Ollie. Have you had a paycheck before?"

His brow furrowed. "I got rolls."

"Well, those are kind of an extra. A bonus. But I need to pay you and I should do it properly even if it is for just an hour or less a day. But I don't have your Social Security number. Do you have an account at the bank where you could deposit a check?"

He stared at her blankly. "Barry pays me sometimes."

"So he would know all this?" She flicked a glance at the clock. The weather had warmed up and now it was raining, a steady, dreary drizzle that had turned the snow to slush and chilled the bones, apparently keeping her usual morning customers at home. "If you could either wait or come back in an hour or so, I could close for a bit and we could run up to the greenhouse to talk to him. Is that okay with you?"

Ollie nodded, already blissfully in the thrall of his favorite confection.

"And then maybe we could check on a different

coat for you. There's a nice consignment shop in town and—"

Her cell phone rang. She pulled it from her pocket, glanced at the incoming area code and flipped it open as she headed for the privacy of the kitchen. "Grandpa Pete! It's great to hear from you."

He chuckled. "I was off on a weekend cruise and just got back. Whoo-ee, I got more sun than I bargained for. I'm red as those Indian paintbrush flowers you always liked. So how's everything at the store?"

He sounded so relaxed, so happy, that she hesitated. "Fine, all fine. Though I was wondering…how well you know Barry Hubble?"

Gramps was one of the strongest Christians she knew. He took his faith seriously, walked the walk every day and had always been careful not to judge others.

Judge not, lest ye be judged had been his familiar refrain to her, delivered with a sad shake of his head whenever a customer walked out of the store after uttering a tidbit of spiteful gossip.

Now, his silence told her that he was trying to come up with the right answer within the bounds of his personal code of honor, and that with Barry, it wasn't easy.

"Be careful," he said finally.

"Why?"

"Just trust me."

"Can you be just a *little* more specific?"

"He's a man," Gramps said at last, "who doesn't hesitate to go after what he wants."

"You mean he's dishonest?"

"I didn't say that."

"But he might not stop at ordinary means to get what he's after?"

"Maybe. He isn't one to take no for an answer."

"And what about Ollie?"

"Not a mean bone in that man's body. And despite all his struggles, he's as happy one day as the next. We should all be that lucky. I only wish he'd let the county help him out more."

"With food? Medical care?"

"All of that. I'm also afraid that some winter he's going to freeze to death in that drafty old house of his, but he's just too stubborn to move."

"There," Ollie said, pointing a stubby finger at the road ahead. "Go there."

"Thanks. I don't think I've been here before." She slowed, turned and made her way past a discreet, elegant sign for Mountain View Florist.

The lane wound through a stand of pines, then opened up into a meadow with a long, single-story log building in the middle, and three greenhouses to one side. Several cars were parked in front.

The rest of the area was neatly divided into split-rail fenced sections for separating types of nursery stock, though only a few forlorn trees remained.

Surprised, she surveyed the well-kept facilities. "I didn't expect this," she muttered under her breath.

Ollie nodded. "Barry's."

When she'd first seen Barry at Millie's, he'd looked like an ex-con. Like someone who spelled trouble, and after his gruff announcement that he'd been trying to buy her grandfather's property, she'd let her imagination run a little wild about what he might do to get it.

Now all of those preconceptions were beginning to fade.

A woman stepped out of the log building with a large flower arrangement swathed in plastic, and then Barry himself came out in a yellow slicker with the hood pulled up to help her maneuver the flowers into her car.

Mission accomplished, he strolled over to Erin's car. "Can I help you?"

She rolled down her window and blinked at a gust of rain that blew in. "I just have some questions, if you have a minute."

He braced a hand on the roof and leaned down to peer inside her car at Ollie. "What's happenin'?"

"Got a job. With money."

"Is that so." Barry pursed his lips and nodded. "Come on in. I just have one other customer, and then I'll be right with you."

Inside, the building was fragrant with the scent of flowers, pine and fresh black earth. A wall of glass-fronted coolers were filled with a variety of cut flowers and arrangements, while houseplants, garden supplies and lawn furniture took up the remaining space.

Barry gestured toward a door behind the register, which opened to an office, then motioned them to the two chairs facing his cluttered desk.

Erin told him about Ollie's part-time job at the store, adding that she wanted to give him a proper paycheck.

"Good luck." Barry leaned way back in his chair and crossed one booted foot over the opposite knee. "I just give him cash. He doesn't have a bank account and couldn't keep it straight, anyway. I'm not even sure if he has a Social Security number. If you can track somebody down who the works for the county-welfare system, you can ask them, though."

"I'll do that. It might be good for Ollie to learn these things."

Barry rocked forward and folded his arms on his desk. "So now you're going to be Ms. Social Worker."

For all his nice surroundings, he was still the same creepy Barry she'd first met at her store. "I thought you've been his friend for a long time."

"I help him in my own way. He comes here when he wants to. I let him earn some money. But I can't help every hard-luck case that walks in the door. Can you?"

She had a feeling that when Ollie came here to earn money, the one who benefited the most was Barry. She stood. "I guess I'd like to make a difference, even if it's just one person at a time. Ollie? Shall we go?"

He looked back and forth between the two of them, chewing his full lower lip, then shook his head.

"You don't want a ride somewhere? I could take you home."

"And I'll bet you don't even know where that is," Barry said. "Have you been there? Have you seen how he lives?" The man stared at her through narrowed eyes. "Take him home and take a good look. Security is everything when you have almost nothing—and the county does nothing for you. I oughta know—been there, done that, when I was a kid."

He picked up the pack of cigarettes on his desk and shook one out. "So take a good look, then ask yourself what's better in his view—the devil you know or the devil you don't? He's been able to come here for years, if he needed. Do-gooders like you just come and go."

"My grandfather said he was worried about Ollie's house during the winter—that it's too cold."

Barrie shrugged. "He's got a wood-burning furnace. He knows how to run it." He gestured toward the door with a flick of his wrist. "Go with her, Ollie. Let her take you home."

Unsettled, Erin led the way to her car and opened

the door for Ollie. "You can stay here if you want to, it's your choice."

He gave her a hunted look. "Barry said."

"That doesn't mean you have to *do* what he says. Does he make you do a lot of things? Does he ever tell you to do things that you don't want to do?"

Ollie climbed in her car and averted his face.

"If that ever happens, you can trust me. I'll help you in whatever way I can. Understand?"

He didn't answer.

Could it be possible, despite his apparently up-standing place in the community, that Barry might still be the one behind her problems at the store? Did he covet Gramps's property enough that he'd try to drive her away using a simple, trusting man to do his dirty work in order to keep his own name clear?

She glanced over at the gentle giant of a man sitting next to her, taking in the lines of worry etching his face.

And hoped it wasn't true.

The farther she drove south of town, the greater her disbelief—and her uneasiness. "Ollie, are you *sure* this is the right way? You really live out this far? And yet you walk clear to the store?"

He nodded, not meeting her eyes.

Thoughts of too-stupid-to-live characters in movies started flashing through her mind. The ones who would go down into creepy basements in the middle of the night, a fading flashlight in hand. Or climb rickety stairs to the attic of an abandoned house—and then meet their doom.

Going this far out in the country with Ollie suddenly seemed like a remarkably bad idea, despite Barry's challenge.

She'd slowed, ready to pull onto the shoulder and turn around, when Ollie pointed a stubby finger at a crumbling house in the distance. "There."

Even from here, she could see that the front porch hung at a tipsy angle and most of the paint had peeled away. Junker cars were parked haphazardly in the yard. Worse, some of the windows on the second floor were broken, and she could see that Ollie had stuffed the holes with rags, then covered them with cardboard from the inside. Even if he closed off the upper floor, what must that house be like in the middle of a good Montana winter?

Yet, as she drove on, she could see that an old-fashioned, hand-powered push mower was leaning against the house and that most of the weeds had been held at bay. And though the yard was like an automotive graveyard, there was no litter there, no trash heaped just outside the door.

Despite everything, Ollie was trying to make the house a decent place to live.

She pulled over onto the shoulder of the highway and stopped by the mailbox out front. "This is your home?"

He nodded, flags of bright color staining his pale cheeks.

"Do you live all alone?"

A single nod.

"Who cooks for you?"

He didn't answer.

"Who brings you food?"

"A lady, sometimes. Boxes and boxes."

"It looks like you must do a very, very good job with the grass in the summer. And you keep everything picked up, too. Could I see the inside sometime?"

He vehemently shook his head as he opened the car door and climbed out.

She watched him trudge up the rutted driveway. Four fat, gleaming cats appeared from behind a rickety shed and bounded over to him, winding through his ankles until they all disappeared into the house together.

She sank back in the seat, her heart heavy, and thought about his childlike wonder at simple caramel rolls and coffee. The determination it took to make such a long trip to work for just an hour.

Where was the county in all this? The social workers? Where was the safe and clean and decent housing that a county ought to provide for unfortunates like him?

Ollie deserved better, and she was going to follow through and see that he got it. No matter what Barry Hubble thought.

THIRTEEN

Jack drummed his fingers on the steering wheel of his car and stared at the nearly deserted main drag of Lost Falls.

On the positive side, the salesman from the security company in Red Lodge had arrived this morning and was meeting with Erin.

On the negative, a phone call from Jack's secretary in Texas had revealed disturbing news.

The investigation into Ted's missing funds wasn't going well. Though Ted had stolen funds mostly from his elderly clients—probably assuming they'd be less likely to realize what was going on—some of them had relatives who were influential businessmen and were riled, demanding justice.

And now the investigators were back to delving into Jack's side of the business.

Jack had been scrupulously honest. His own stable of investors had been safe. But how long would it take for a frustrated investigator to find—or even fabricate—some link that could tie Jack to Ted's schemes? And given Ted's propensity for lies, it might not be too difficult. The man had probably laid a very careful trail that led straight to Jack's door.

After dropping Max off at Isabelle's place to play with the other children, Jack drove to a coffee shop where the Internet connection, though far slower than his cable back home, was still better than what he had at the rental house.

He would continue his own investigation until he figured out what Ted had done with the stolen money, if it was the last thing he ever did. And he would make sure Ted's clients got back every penny.

After months of worry and frustration, however, he was growing less optimistic the longer he tried. None of his hunches had panned out so far. He was no closer to recovering the money now than when he'd first learned about Ted's betrayal. Would it ever be over?

The first day Ted hadn't shown up at the office, Jack had just assumed the man had taken the day to work from home. But as one day followed the next, Jack grew worried. He went to Ted's condo and pounded on the door, then called the police, fearing Ted was ill…or worse.

The pile of mail beneath the mail slot, the emptied

drawers hanging half-open in the bedroom and the soured milk in a glass on the counter had made it clear that he was gone.

The increasingly agitated phone calls from Ted's clients had made something else clear—that he'd managed to empty many of those accounts before fleeing.

Before contacting the authorities, Jack had photocopied account numbers. Banking information. Every possible lead, or contact name, and even a list of passwords Ted had kept hidden under the blotter on his desk.

Sure enough, the investigators had boxed up Ted's files and taken them all away, but at least Jack had something to go on.

But nothing had panned out. Yet.

Settling in an isolated corner of the quaint shop with his laptop and a latte, he pulled a dog-eared paper from his billfold, carefully smoothed it out on the table and surveyed the list of possible leads that he'd typed out before leaving Texas.

Erin's lovely face slipped into his thoughts. With those startling, light blue eyes and all that silky blond hair, she looked fragile as spun glass, yet he'd never met another woman with more independence and determination.

He found himself smiling as he thought about her crazy pup and how she'd thought the big galoot was going to be a watchdog to protect her. From chipmunks, maybe.

But his humor faded as he surveyed the dwindling number of possible leads he had to go on. Ted had probably been too smart to leave a trail.

Maybe he'd even left these clues on purpose, to sidetrack anyone trying to investigate. And maybe that money was gone forever into unknown accounts, and with it, any chance for Jack to prove once and for all that he'd had no part in Ted's schemes.

A rusty prayer hovered on his lips. *Hey, God, I could really use some help here. Ted's clients are suffering. My office staff will be jobless if I go under. And if I'm implicated in this mess, who will be there for Max? There's no one else for him. Please, God, tell me what to do.*

No matter what, he and Max would need to go back to Texas after his lease was up in Montana. He would need to find a way to rebuild his career, so he could establish a stable, comfortable home for Max.

But in the process, he would have to leave Erin behind.

Though his feelings for her had been steadily deepening, he didn't have to ask her to know what the answer would be if he asked her to move to Texas for a chance to continue their relationship.

She would want to stay here and honor her commitment to her grandfather. But more than that, what kind of gamble would that be, moving more than a thousand miles to follow a guy who might eventually be facing prison? He couldn't let that happen.

So he would keep his feelings firmly in check and keep his distance. She deserved far better than someone like him.

The tiny library in Lost Falls was housed in an old brick bungalow on Main Street, its bookshelves crammed into what had once been the bedrooms, living room and dining area. The "tech center," set up in the former kitchen, housed a typewriter and two computers that were dinosaurs from the late 1980s with dial-up Internet access.

Erin fidgeted on the swivel stool as yet another page from the Birch Valley newspaper archives slowly loaded onto the screen.

"Hey, Lily," she called out. "When are you guys putting in cable?"

"Never." The librarian, a middle-aged woman with a cheery smile, shuffled into the room, a hot cup of mint tea in her hand.

"That's not soon enough. Hey, I like your shoes, by the way." The woman's conservative navy pantsuit was certainly standard fare, compared to her bright red furry slippers.

"The slippers and tea are the only way I can keep

warm in this place." She lifted her mug. "Can I make you some?"

Erin looked up at the old-fashioned clock on the wall. "I'd better get back to the store, but thanks, anyway."

"You know, it's quiet here today. I'd be glad to continue searching for whatever you're trying to find."

"Really? Thanks!" Erin jotted down the dates she was researching and the name of the park. "I've been looking at the Birch Valley paper so far, but haven't even started on the *Denver Post*. I'm looking for anything suspicious in the area to the north or west of Denver. Missing people, murders, maybe even a major drug deal."

"Wow. Heavy stuff."

"It's just that I was in a state park and saw someone—or something—from afar. It's been bothering me ever since, but I'm hoping that it was just my imagination."

Lily shivered and cradled her mug with both hands. "I hope that person didn't see *you*. That could be bad. Of course, you live way up here now. So that's lucky."

"Definitely."

Except…a smart, *desperate* man had the world at his fingertips these days. With a little sleuthing he could've found out her name—maybe even from someone cleaning up after the wedding.

People searches were a breeze on the Internet and

would be an easy ticket to a world of information—
even her old address. And Ashley's door.

A knot of fear settled in the pit of her stomach. "I—
I have to go. Please, do call if you find anything, okay?"

At Millie's, Erin unlocked the front door and took
Charlie out of his kennel to let him run in the fenced
yard in back. By the time she came inside, the phone
was ringing.

"I'm not sure if this is what you're looking for, but
there's an ongoing investigation into the disappearance
of a guy who owns a chain of dry cleaners. He was last
seen alive around the time of your friend's wedding.'

"Really?"

"There've been a couple of articles on it. Otherwise,
there were some gang-related shootings and domestic
disputes, but none of those victims are missing. I
printed the articles for you—do you have a fax?"

Erin rattled off the number. "I can't tell you how
much I appreciate this, Lily. If you stop by sometime,
there'll be a caramel roll and cup of coffee for you
on the house."

A few customers came in for coffee to go, then
left. Erin paced anxiously near the fax machine, then
jumped when it finally rang.

Eight pages came through, a little grainy, but clear
enough to read. Shuffling them together, she headed
for the corner table in the café and began to read.

The first articles showed a photo of the missing businessman, a Ronald Peterson. The others included quotes by the investigators, who were at a loss as to where Peterson could be.

When she turned to the last one, her heart stumbled. *The missing man's body had been found buried in an unnamed park, but there were no suspects in his murder.*

And in this article, there were photos of the two lead detectives on the case. She squinted at the photos, trying to make out the details.

Her nerves jangling, Erin reached for her cell and speed-dialed a number. *Come on, Ashley, pick up.* But it rang eight times, then went into voice mail.

And Erin started to pray.

FOURTEEN

A steady trickle of customers came into the store through the afternoon. Familiar faces, now. People who asked about her grandfather or called Charlie by name and leaned down to scratch him behind the ears.

The usual trio of elderly Second World War vets who often showed up around four to have coffee by the warmth of the potbellied stove, playing checkers and talking about the war until one by one they noticed the time and headed for home.

Ashley still hadn't called back by five o'clock.

Erin read through the newspaper articles once more, then picked up the phone, dialed for Directory Assistance and called the Birch Valley Police Department.

"I'm…uh…calling about an article I read in the paper. About the body that was found in the park."

"Hold on." The line went dead for a moment, then clicked. "Sergeant Dean."

"I'd like to talk to the person in charge of the Peterson case."

"Your name?" He sounded bored, as if he'd fielded calls from crackpots all week.

"Erin Cole."

"And you have information?"

"I'd like to talk to the investigator who was quoted in the newspaper. Patrick Doyle."

"He's not available, but I can help you just as well."

"Actually, I need to talk to him. If I can leave a message, he could call me back."

The sergeant heaved a sigh. "He's no longer on the case. And before you ask, he's also on a leave of absence. So if you have any information, you're talking to the right guy."

"What does that mean exactly, not on the case?" She could tell the sergeant was becoming irritated with her, but she pressed on. "Would that mean he hadn't been doing a good job with it? Or that he—"

"Look, I can't release that sort of information. If there's anything you need to tell us, please do. If you have some sort of personal issues with Doyle, you'll need to contact him directly."

"I understand from the newspaper article that Peterson was last seen alive in the vicinity of a park near Denver and that he was later found dead." She twisted the phone cord around her index finger. "I think I may have some photographs you'd like to see."

"Photographs? Of what?"

"Possibly of someone who was involved. It's just a guess, but I really need to show these pictures to somebody."

"Can you drop them by the police station? Or do you need an officer to stop by and pick them up?"

"I'm actually in Montana. But I was in that park for a wedding on the approximate day that man was murdered."

"Right. So you got a picture of the murderer just by chance?"

He still didn't believe her. "I've been researching this case by using the Internet to go through old newspaper archives. I didn't realize until just recently that I had pictures that might mean something. None of the articles reveal the exact location of where that body was buried, right?"

"That information hasn't been shared with the press, ma'am."

"Well, I think it was about fifteen yards from the river, back in an undeveloped part of the park just north of Birch Valley. I saw the remnants of an old, abandoned settlers' cabin close by."

The sergeant fell silent.

"And something else—I was on the other side of that river at the time, where there's an overgrown fire road. That's how I happened to be back there, after attending a friend's wedding."

"Give me your name and address, please." The man's voice was sharp, alert and all business. "And the best telephone number to use for reaching you."

She gave him the information. "Do you want me to send prints?"

"I'd like you to send them directly to me by e-mail attachment. Do you know how to do that?"

"No problem. I can probably do it on Sunday or Monday, when I get my pictures back from the drugstore. There'll be a CD with the prints."

He carefully spelled out his e-mail address. "I'll be watching for them. In the meantime, one of our investigators may give you a call to ask questions about what you saw."

She hesitated, debating whether to share her suspicions about the identity of the man she'd seen in the woods. But if the sergeant thought she was trying to pin the blame on one of their own, he might discount her entire story. Who would believe her, after all?

"Thanks. I'll do anything I can to help."

After hanging up, she felt a cold chill work its way down her spine.

Someone had been searching her property.

Her laptop was missing.

Until now, she'd suspected Barry of trying to subtly intimidate her. He'd made no bones about wanting her property and his hopes that she would sell.

But what if she really *had* caught a killer in those photos, and he'd tracked her here, trying to retrieve them?

She'd never uploaded the photos onto the computer. If he was the one who had stolen it, he'd know that by now.

And he'd definitely be back.

The call from Dean came at seven o'clock, and it was the call Patrick had feared for more than a month.

"She's probably one of those crazies, you know," he scoffed, switching his cell phone to his other ear. "Maybe she even staged some pictures, hoping to get her name in the newspapers."

"She sounded normal to me. And she also described the area where the body was buried. That information hasn't been leaked to the press, and there were no bystanders around when we processed the scene. She *had* to be there."

Patrick felt his palms grow damp. "Is someone going after the pictures?"

"This is the crazy part. She says she's up in Montana, but she'll e-mail them in a few days. I just hope they don't disappear in cyberspace. If she's right about them, she could help blow this case wide-open."

"Don't get your hopes up," Patrick said easily. "Sounds like just another dead end to me."

"But one we can't ignore. Given Peterson's drug affiliations, his killer was probably a buyer or a supplier."

"Maybe the perp did everyone a favor, getting rid of the guy."

"But finding who offed Peterson could lead us straight up the ladder. This call is off the record of course. I still think it was wrong to take you off the case, and I just thought you'd like to hear how things are going."

Staring at the endless ribbon of asphalt leading to Lost Falls, Patrick gripped the phone long after his old friend ended the call, his stomach twisting in a tight knot and his hands shaking.

He'd volunteered to head up the investigation into Peterson's death, hoping he could do subtle damage control and intercept anything that might tie him to the case.

But he'd known it was only a matter of time when he'd caught the curious looks. The pointed questions. The murmurs behind his back. Complaints about the so-called "flaws" in his investigative procedures had dogged him every step of the way.

Being removed from the case had been humiliating. Yesterday's intense questioning, followed by being placed on administrative leave, had made his future crystal clear.

The other homicide detectives were quietly gathering evidence against him, but they didn't have a tight case—yet. As lcng as he kept those pictures out of their hands, he still had a chance.

And already, the lights of Lost Falls were coming into view.

FIFTEEN

"Sorry about the late call, but I figured you'd still be up if I phoned before eleven. It was great hearing your message." Ashley laughed. "In fact, I looked at my calendar as soon as I listened to it, trying to decide when I can come up for a visit. I think some of our other friends might want to come along, too, if that's okay."

"I'd love it. I won't have much room for guests until the middle of December, but after my renter leaves I'll probably really wish I had some company. It'll seem awfully quiet here when he's gone."

"Ahh. So he's ended up being a pretty interesting guy? Tell me more!"

"Ashley—"

"Come on, you can tell Auntie Ashley. Since my social life is so dull right now, maybe I can vicariously enjoy yours."

Erin felt a sinking sensation in the pit of her stomach. "What about that handsome cop who stopped by after your car was damaged? He sounded pretty cool."

Ashley snorted. "I must hold the record for having the shortest relationships on the planet. He was here for an hour and he really was sweet. I was sure he was interested and he said he would call. But he never did."

"If you saw a picture of him, would you recognize him?"

"Are you kidding? He was the kind of guy you dream of, with those dark good looks of his. And his smile…" Ashley sighed.

"Is your fax machine working yet?"

Ashley gave a startled laugh. "No, I still need to take it back to the store for service. Why?"

"I need to send you a newspaper article, see if you recognize the picture of the investigator. I'm wondering if it's the same guy."

Ashley fell silent for a moment. "Bob is a cop, so I imagine he would be involved in all sorts of cases. That wouldn't be unusual."

"You know the little business office in the condo complex for the residents' use? It should be open until midnight, so I'm sending a fax to that number. I need you to take a look and let me know if you think it's the same guy. It's important. Just call me back at the number for Millie's as soon as you can, and I'll wait up for you. My cell battery is nearly dead and it isn't taking a charge very well."

Erin walked across the store to the fax machine behind the cash register, tapped the photocopies of the articles into a neat stack and settled them into the machine. Studying the condo-association business card she'd found in her wallet, she dialed the fax number.

The pages slowly fed through the machine, then Erin started to pace the floor. The second hand dragged slowly, slowly, slowly around the wall clock above the cash register.

A little after midnight, the phone jangled. Erin picked it up before the second ring. "Do you have them yet?"

"Sorry it took so long. The door was locked and I had to call Maintenance." Ashley took a shaky breath. "I…I just don't understand. It's Bob, all right, though they made a mistake. That's not his name under the photo. But then, newspapers do that all the time. They're always putting in little apologies on the inside of the front page, saying they've gotten names or addresses wrong—"

"*Ashley.*" Erin sank into one of the café chairs and rested her forehead on her open palm. "I don't think it's a mistake. I'm guessing there was never a random vandal breaking into your car. And I'm also guessing the damage was a ruse to get into your condo so he could track me down."

"But he seemed so nice!" Ashley's voice was

breathless, weak. "And why wouldn't he just ask for your address?"

"Maybe so you wouldn't get suspicious and then tell me about it. Or maybe he knew that no smart woman would give out another woman's address."

"B-but he didn't say *anything* about you. And why would he need to find you so badly?"

"You left right after Linda's wedding ceremony, but I stayed later and took a lot of shots throughout the park. I inadvertently captured a guy in the woods. I don't think he was out there having a picnic."

"These articles you sent. They're about some murder victim named Ronald Peterson." Ashley fell silent for a moment and then added, "It says that he's suspected of having a connection to a drug ring, and that he might've used his businesses as a cover." She drew in a deep breath. "And you think my Bob—or Patrick or whoever he is—was involved?"

"I don't know why or how. I only know that I used a long, telephoto lens in the park, so my pictures weren't entirely clear. The fax is a little grainy, as well. But if I had to guess, I'd say Patrick Doyle and Bob are the same guy—and that I caught him on film at the worst possible moment near the murder scene. You should see the look of rage on his face when he realized I was there with a camera."

"Look closer at your photos." Ashley's voice rose, tinged with panic. "Maybe you're wrong."

"I sent my memory card away to have prints made, so I don't have the pictures handy right now. But I think your 'friend' gave you a false name. And I think he did it so he could track me down. Earlier you said you had to look for your car registration, so that left him alone in the kitchen. Maybe he saw my forwarding address taped to your refrigerator, or looked at the address book you keep by the phone. Maybe he even casually asked about your roommates, and you mentioned the town I was moving to. There's been trouble up here, Ash."

"Oh, no. Erin, I'm so sorry. I didn't have any idea!"

"I don't know for sure if it's him, but—"

The phone went dead.

Startled, Erin pulled the receiver away from her ear and stared at it, then slowly cradled it.

From somewhere in the back of the store came the sound of a single, deliberate footstep.

And then the lights went out.

Jack palmed his cell phone and thought about calling Erin, then glanced out his living-room window. The lights were off in the store, so she'd probably gone back to the cottage. His call could wait.

He stared pensively out the window, wondering what she would say when he told her the whole truth.

She'd once asked why he happened to choose Lost

Falls, and he'd said that he'd looked on the Internet for places to stay in the Montana Rockies. True.

But he'd also headed in this direction because of a scrap of paper he'd found on the floor next to a wastebasket, when he and a police officer had first entered Ted's apartment.

"Lost Falls" had been scrawled on it, then scratched out.

He'd called it to the attention of the deputy and then to the investigators who took on the case later, but apparently no one had followed up. Or if they had, they'd only checked on Ted's real name with the Montana authorities.

But when Jack did a city-and-zip-code check and found that the only town of Lost Falls in the entire country was in Montana, it was a lead he couldn't ignore.

Now, he paced the living-room floor, then stopped at his desk to pull out a state map.

Unfurling it, he spread it wide and studied the towns circled in red ink. Six towns he'd visited in the past few days. He'd taken posters that he'd made with his computer and printer, and had shown it to some of the locals in each town.

He'd come up dry in the first five.

But today he'd finally hit pay dirt at the Copper Cliff post office and at a little string of cabins tucked in the woods.

Apparently there'd been a man in town who closely resembled Ted, though he'd worn a hat tipped low over his face and had the start of a beard.

The postmistress had sworn she never forgot a face and said he looked familiar—he was the only person she'd ever dealt with who wanted to buy a single stamp with a hundred-dollar bill.

The elderly gentleman at the cabins had been hesitant, but his wife had taken one look and nodded, her mouth flattening to a grim line. "That's him. He was here and he paid in cash, but he won't be back. Not over my dead body."

Her husband had pursed his lips and frowned at her, but she'd continued, anyway, "He didn't like the pillows and he didn't like the towels. Nothing was good enough. Hardly left the cabin, stayed in there to eat, because he left food wrappers everywhere. What kind of vacation is that, after coming all the way up here?"

Knowing that the local banks wouldn't release information to him, this afternoon Jack had contacted the police department back home with the name Ted had likely used while he was up here and the names of the towns nearby. Had Ted divvied up the stolen money to put into a number of rural banks, using false identities?

"It won't be long, Ted," he muttered under his breath as he paced the living room, knowing sleep wouldn't come easily tonight. "And the day your schemes are unraveled will be a day I'll remember for the rest of my life."

Erin took a step backward, feeling for the edge of the table. Her heart battering against her ribs, she held her breath and waited for her eyes to adjust to the dark, monochrome shadows in the store.

The moon was only a sliver tonight, and its faint wash of light barely picked out the silhouettes of the display cases and the soda fountain.

Again she heard a subtle movement.

Clutching her keys in one hand, she judged the distance to the front door. It wasn't locked yet. If she got there in time, she could jerk it open and run.

But anyone at the back of the store would have about the same distance to run as she did—if he was after her and not just wanting to empty the cash register.

The thought made her stomach pitch. *Lord, help me—tell me what to do.*

"I know you're here," a voice crooned through the darkness. "I watched you through the window for a long time. Did you know that? Did you *feel* it? You're so beautiful, with all that silky blond hair. I've watched you—a lot."

She inched toward the front door, crouching low. Could he hear her crazy heartbeat? Could he see her shadowed form in the darkness? *Please, God, help me get out of here. Please, God...*

"You have something I need," he continued in that same, eerie, singsong voice. "If you cooperate I'll leave, and you'll never see me again. That's easy, isn't it?"

The door was ten feet away.

Nine.

Eight.

She could almost feel the coolness of the old-fashioned knob beneath her palm.

Seven.

The muscles in her thighs burned as she crept forward, still crouching low. She held her breath, trying not to make a sound.

It was there—just within reach. *Please, God. Please, God. Please—*

A callused hand clamped her wrist and in one, fierce motion, twisted it high behind her back until agonizing pain rocketed through her shoulder and her knees collapsed.

She screamed.

And then everything went black.

Jack tucked the covers up around Max's shoulders and stepped out of the room.

In minutes the child was out of bed again, his eyes spilling tears.

At Isabelle's he'd reportedly been tired and

cranky, with flushed cheeks and watery eyes, and things had gone downhill from there.

Rather than stopping at Millie's to tell Erin the news about his trip to Copper Cliff, Jack had taken Max home and tried putting him to bed as Isabelle had suggested.

"Probably just a flu bug," she'd said. "All the kids have been getting it, but it only lasts a day or so. If you need any help, just give me a call, and I'll come over," she'd added with a knowing smile. "Moms are used to this sort of thing. But for a first-timer, it can be tough dealing with a sick child."

She'd been offhand about the flu, but Max had steadily become more whiny, refused everything Jack offered for supper, then fought his bath time and the books that usually followed. By midnight he'd thrown up twice, and for the last half hour he'd been on the couch looking miserable and listless.

"I want my doggie," he whined, tears welling up in his eyes and his lower lip trembling. "I need my doggie."

At least this time, it was something Jack could provide, unlike a tearful, heartbreaking request for his mommy. "I'll look, okay?"

But the stuffed animal wasn't in the main-floor bedrooms, the office or hidden in a corner of the living room. A search of the car proved fruitless, as well. "Do you have any idea where it could be?"

The boy burst into tears.

"You didn't take it to Isabelle's, did you?" They'd set a strict rule about that after Max had left it behind on his first day at the woman's house.

Max shook his head, his little body racked with sobs.

Jack sat next to him on the couch and rested the back of his hand against the boy's forehead. *Cool, thank goodness.* "Do you know where else it could be?"

"I—I took it to see Charlie."

Jack reached for his cell phone to dial Erin's number, then remembered the time. "I can't call her now. She'll be sleeping."

"I need my doggie. I can't sleep without him!"

Doggie, and a chance to sleep.

No doggie, and whining all night.

The options were clear and so was the answer.

Jack stood and went to the window once again. Maybe Erin was at the cottage but still awake. Surely she'd understand the needs of a sick and miserable little boy.

Odd. If he stood at a certain angle, he could catch a glimpse of the cottage. It was dark—even the porch light that she always left on at night. As if she'd never come home.

And suddenly some lights were on again, at the back of the store. Why would she be there at this hour? And if she'd returned to the store, why weren't the cottage porch lights on to light her way?

An uneasy sensation spider-crawled up his neck.

"Please, can I go get my doggie?" Max's plaintive voice cut through Jack's thoughts. "I'll get it myself—I don't mind."

"I don't want you going over there, buddy. You're sick."

"But—"

"I'll get it. It'll just take me a little while." He flipped out his cell phone and punched in a number. *Sorry, Isabelle, but you did offer. I hope a fifty-dollar tip will be enough.*

If someone was here with Max, Jack could fetch the stuffed animal and then talk to Erin for a while. Make sure she was all right. Maybe even ask her the questions he'd been wanting to ask.

But then he lifted his gaze to the store once more, and that uneasy sensation increased ten times over. Those lights in the back were never left on at night. He could see jerky shadows moving against the wall.

Shadows. Not just one.

Something wasn't right. He could feel it in his bones.

"Isabelle. I need you over here ASAP to stay with Max for a few minutes. I need to check on Erin. Please hurry."

And as soon as he ended the call, he dialed 911.

SIXTEEN

Erin fought the nausea welling up in her throat. The searing pain in her shoulder had settled into steady throbbing, given the way her hands were tied so tightly behind her back.

But worse than the pain was the fact that she knew the face in front of her all too well. And he didn't care. He'd made no effort to disguise himself—which meant he planned to kill her, whether she cooperated or not.

What she needed was time.

She needed to figure a way out of this.

God willing, she'd have an opportunity to enjoy her new life here, and to grow old and gray and content, with dozens of grandchildren at her feet. *Please, God, send someone to help me.*

"You know what I'm after," Patrick said with an eerie smile. "You must have known from the very first moment that you were wrong to take those photos. Is that why you disappeared so fast? You knew you'd better run?"

He watched her for a moment, his head tilted, as if honestly amused by and curious about her lack of compliance. Then he glanced around and grabbed a baseball bat from several displayed in an old cream can.

"You sell everything in this store, don't you," he marveled. In one fluid motion he rose, hefted the bat, then spun around and swung the bat against the corner of the bench she was sitting on, just inches away, shattering the bat. "A little misjudgment and that could've been your knee, sweet Erin. My guess is that you'd never walk on it again. Not that it'll be an issue, anyway, should you choose to be stubborn."

He leaned over and casually pulled another bat from the display. He studied it with admiration, stroking its smoothly polished surface. "So beautiful. Just. Like. You."

Again he coiled into a powerful batter's stance, but this time he swung full force at the wall of glass-fronted coolers. The glass exploded, sending shards of lethal missiles across the room.

She flinched as the glass splinters sliced into her upper arm and cheek, sending blood flowing hot and thick down her arm and neck.

"The lights were all off at the house next door when I arrived, so there's no one around to hear you if you scream, sweetheart. No one is going to save you."

Patrick pulled up a chair, spun it and sat on it backward, his arms folded across the top. "I'm impatient, Erin. I hate to desecrate a lovely face like yours. But I'll do whatever it takes, because I need your camera, the memory card and every hard copy you have of those photos you took at the park. Understand?"

She surreptitiously twisted her hands, trying to gain slack in the tight cord binding them. *Keep him talking. Keep him distracted—anything to gain more time.*

"W-was it you who broke into the store?" The cord slipped a few millimeters.

He sighed. "And your cottage, of course. Once I got your laptop, I discovered the photos hadn't been uploaded, so it was useless. And I couldn't find your camera—until I saw you take it out of the trunk of your car the day you went sledding. You've made this very difficult."

"I would've given them to you if you'd asked." She struggled to keep herself still and her expression neutral while fighting the cord. Again, it loosened, just a hair. Blood rushed back into her fingers.

Looming over her, he uttered a harsh curse. "Then do it."

"I will—when I get the prints and memory card back." She tried to quell the shaking of her voice. "Y-you can have it all. I'll hand the sealed envelope to you without even opening it."

He stalked to the front of the store and then came back and towered over her, his fists clenched. "What do you mean, when you get it back?"

"I dropped the card in a mailer and sent it off at the drugstore. It went out to someplace in California on Monday and will take at least seven days to come back. But it's cheaper that way and—"

"Monday?" he roared. The veins bulged at his temples and he swore again. His eyes narrowed. "But I hardly need you to go get them now that I know where they'll be, and when."

"The drugstore owners are old friends of my family. They'll be suspicious if anyone else tries to pick up a packet with my name."

His laugh was pure evil. "Oh, please. In this Podunk town? I'll have no trouble with a little after-hours pickup—*without* their help."

"But if anything happens to me, they'll remember the photos. They'll be eager to tell the police, hoping there'll be clues among the photos I took. So the police will intercept the package for sure."

He pulled back a fist and slammed it into the side of her face. Pain exploded through her head in a dizzying explosion of stars. "Someone smart as you oughta know when to keep her pretty mouth shut. You know what? Maybe you and me will go for a little drive. Far as everyone knows, you'll be off visiting a sick uncle. I'll even put a note in the store window to tell them—and once I collect my photos it won't matter *what* anyone finds."

He grabbed her elbow and jerked her to her feet. "Let's go."

If she went through that door, she knew it would be over. There'd be no more chances. She glanced wildly back and forth, searching for an escape route. A weapon. If only she could free her hands.

"Ohh," she moaned, letting her knees buckle and her body fall like dead weight to the floor. Caught off balance, Patrick stumbled into a stacked display of soda 24-packs and fell sideways when the display gave way.

He cursed and awkwardly lurched to his feet— close enough that she could coil and slam her hard-soled shoes into the back of his knees with every ounce of strength she possessed.

He fell against the broken glass of the cooler and screamed. "You're *dead,* sister! You hear me?"

Again she wrenched her wrists against her bonds until the cord cut deep into her flesh—but this time, she gained enough slack to free her hands.

Praying he couldn't see her well enough in the shadows on the floor, she grabbed a five-pound bag of ice-cream salt from a bottom shelf near her head and ripped a wide hole in the plastic.

From the corner of her eye she saw a flash of movement outside the window. Someone heading for the back door. *Jack?* Or did Patrick have an accomplice? *Let it be Jack, Lord. Please, let it be Jack.*

Patrick staggered back to her, and even in the dim light she could see the blood dripping from his hands and the gash on his cheek. *"Get up!"*

"I…I can't—my shoulder!" She scrambled sideways, moaning. "Please, loosen the rope. It hurts so much!"

"I said, get up!" Patrick screamed, brandishing a small revolver that he'd pulled from his waistband. "Now!"

She saw the faintest crack of light appear through the back door. *Now or never.*

She jumped to her feet and spun around, throwing the salt into Patrick's face. He reeled back, choking and coughing and crying out, clawing at the wound on his face—

And then a massive white form hurtled through the store and launched itself at his back, snarling and snapping, slamming him to the ground. *Charlie?*

The gun exploded as it flew out of Patrick's hand, filling the air with the hot, pungent scent of cordite.

In an instant Jack was there, sweeping up the gun in one hand and training it on Patrick's chest as he reached for the dog's collar with his other hand.

Charlie fought the grip on his collar, then reluctantly backed away, his body rigid and eyes pinned on Patrick as if begging for a chance to attack again.

Blood pooled beneath Patrick's leg. His eyes shifted wildly between the dog and the gun as he clutched at his thigh, writhing in pain.

"Can you hear that? Help is on the way," she said softly, listening to the sound of approaching sirens. She moved over to take hold of Charlie's collar. "You're lucky, Patrick, because this dog would really like to tear you apart, and I just hate to deprive him of such pleasure."

Patrick scrabbled away from Charlie until his back hit the wall. "You wouldn't…you wouldn't let him."

"Of course not. I think the courts will have a heyday deciding on the future you deserve."

"You got nothing on me."

"Sounds like murder and attempted murder to me," Jack said mildly. "Just for starters." He glanced briefly at Erin, then focused on Patrick. "Are you all right?"

She looked up at him, and her heart swelled with emotion until it felt too big for her chest. "I was so afraid you were one of his friends…"

"And I have never prayed so hard in my life."

Swirling lights flooded through the front windows of the store as patrol cars pulled up outside. "Well, it sure must've worked, because I think the cavalry has just arrived."

By the time the sheriff and his deputies completed their paperwork and an ambulance had taken Patrick away, it was nearly two in the morning. Erin still felt as if she was buzzing on an overload of adrenaline.

"I just can't believe it's over," she whispered, leaning against Jack's chest as they sat on the porch swing. Charlie had crawled into her lap and was now draped across both of them, snoring softly. "This sort of thing happens in the movies, not in real life."

"I still think you should've let the EMTs take you to the hospital so you could be checked out."

"I'm fine—just a few cuts and bruises."

"Your shoulder might not be so fine."

"Right now, I'm just sort of numb all over. I knew he planned to kill me, and when I thought I saw you coming, I was terrified that you might walk through the door and he'd shoot you, as well."

"And he would have if you hadn't distracted him." Jack tucked her closer into his embrace and kissed her cheek. Charlie whined in his sleep, his paws pedaling briefly as if he, too, was reliving the terrifying evening. "It's sort of ironic that Patrick is the only one who was shot and that he did it to himself."

She ruffled Charlie's fur. "I guess the three of us make a good team."

"But God was right with us, too."

Surprised, she looked up at him. "I thought you two weren't on speaking terms."

Jack's mouth tipped into a wry grin. "I'm sure God was still trying to speak to me. It was me who was holding the grudge. After Janie's death—" he swallowed "—I had a hard time. But I've never felt God's presence more than I did tonight. It was as if He was with me every step of the way. I was just so afraid I was going to lose you."

"I was praying at the same time, believe me." She threaded her fingers through his. "For your safety and for Patrick to make some kind of error that would stop him before it was too late."

Jack stroked the dog's fluffy white fur. "Charlie helped with that."

"So I had two heroes tonight," she teased.

"I'm just glad Max fell asleep before Isabelle even arrived. He'll never even have to know what happened."

"Is he still sleeping?"

"When I last checked, he was, and Isabelle was snoozing on the couch under an afghan or two. I think I'll just let her stay there till morning so she can get a good night's rest."

Erin looked up at the brilliant stars strewn across the black velvet sky. "How is your investigation coming along?"

"I've found some possible links to offshore accounts that Ted might have set up, but also found out that he was seen in Copper Cliff a few weeks before he died. I'd guess he came up here to go into hiding and filter some of the money into the local banks under false identities, then he panicked. Who knows what he was thinking, but I guess we'll never know. I contacted the sheriff up here and the investigators back in Texas, and they'll be taking over the investigation from here on."

"Shouldn't they have handled it from the beginning?"

"They have—to a degree. But this isn't their only case, and I just couldn't sit back and do nothing, not when Ted managed to nearly destroy everything I'd ever worked for. I knew there'd always be higher-profile cases taking manpower away from this one." Jack shook his head slowly. "None of the authorities even knew he was here in Montana. At least now I can go back and start to clear the name of my company."

Tonight she'd felt terror, and shock, and utter relief. And now a sense of sadness and loss crept around her heart. She tried for a casual smile and hoped he believed it. "So you'll be able to go back to Texas, then. That's wonderful."

He studied her face for a long moment. "I guess so."

She felt a corner of her heart start to fracture at hearing those words spoken aloud.

He had to leave, and she couldn't go—but then, he hadn't asked her to, either. Whatever she might have imagined about the possibilities God could have in store for her with this wonderful, incredibly desirable man, had only been a dream.

Why had God brought something so beautiful into her life, only to take it away?

Erin awoke at six and went to the store to begin cleaning up the mess. Broken glass littered the floor. Merchandise displays had been overturned.

But it was the blood that brought back the horror of the night in vivid relief.

Suddenly feeling faint, she moved to the front door and opened it wide to the crisp, early morning mountain air.

And there was Jack's SUV parked in front of the rental house, like always. Only, all of its doors and the hatchback were open; suitcases and boxes were stacked nearby.

Oh, no. Her heart contracted painfully, leaving a huge, empty place in her chest.

Was he just going to leave the keys on the table and drive away without even a farewell? How had she been so terribly wrong about him, about them both?

Maybe he'd seen the emotion in her face last night and was trying to avoid a messy, emotional confrontation—the embarrassment of a crying, clinging woman trying to hold on to a man who only wanted to leave.

Well, that would never be her.

She leaned a shoulder against the door frame, taking in the progress he'd already made, then turned, carefully relocked the front door and made sure the sign in the window said Closed.

With all of the damage in the store, it might be wise to make a trip to her main supplier up in Billings, because the regular delivery truck wouldn't be coming through this area for almost a week.

And staying around to exchange stilted goodbyes didn't sound like a good idea at all.

SEVENTEEN

Jack eased his SUV onto the two-lane highway leading to Cody. There were no straight routes from Lost Falls to Dallas.

There were more than twelve hundred miles to go.

And the silence in the car was deafening—though the expression on Max's face needed no words.

"Are you hungry?" Jack smiled and cut a glance toward his nephew in the rearview mirror. "I'm sure there must be some good places to eat in Cody."

The child mulishly turned his head to stare out the window at the incredible red bluffs that soared above the highway on both sides.

"We've got another good hour to go, and then I think we'll stop, anyway. What about hamburgers? We haven't seen a fast-food place since we got to Lost Falls."

"I want caramel rolls."

Not the answer Jack had hoped for, but at least the

boy had broken his silence. "I'm sure we can find those, too."

"Not someplace else. Where Charlie and Erin live. And the pony and Iz-bell."

When Jack glanced back again and saw the tears glistening down Max's cheeks, he pulled over into a scenic overlook, got out and opened the back door, knowing exactly how the tyke felt but feeling more at a loss than ever. What could he say that could fix this?

Nothing.

He had to go back to Dallas. They both did, so Ted's mess could be straightened out once and for all. So there'd be a decent income in the future and a secure, comfortable life for Max.

Max was crying in earnest now, the sobs shaking through him and tears pouring down his cheeks.

Jack unbuckled the car seat and Max launched himself into his arms, then rested his wet cheek against Jack's neck. The child's sobs ricocheted through Jack's soul as he embraced him.

A surge of love and protectiveness seemed to come from Jack's very bones as Max melted against him for the first time—with no reservation, trusting him to make things right. "I'm so sorry that you're this sad."

"I—I wanna go back. *Please.* I wanna go back."

The counselor had been dead wrong about this trip. Instead of providing a chance for healing and bonding, the poor kid had become attached to a new place and new people, only to be uprooted yet again.

Jack closed his eyes and held Max tighter. "I know it's hard, buddy. But we have a house back in Texas, remember? And when we get home, we'll find a puppy and a pony there, too. Texas has *lots* of them, I promise. And there are great preschools, so you'll have friends, and we'll find someone nice like Isabelle."

"But not Charlie. And not E-Erin."

The boy was right on that score.

Except that Erin had made it crystal clear that their departure was just an early end to the lease agreement. Nothing more. And though he'd figured he needed just a few weeks back home to take care of business, he'd come to realize that maybe a complete break would be the better course—before it hurt even more to leave.

After Elana's abrupt ending of what he'd thought was a lifetime commitment, he knew when to cut his losses and run.

"We can't go back to Erin's, buddy," Jack said gently.

"You can turn around."

He made it sound so simple. "We have to go to Texas. For my job and our house. Remember the swimming pool in back? And the big trees? You have that nice blue bedroom with the Sponge Bob bed-spread, and all the toys."

It was hard enough to try to explain. But when Max sighed with utter defeat and silently laid his head against Jack's shoulder, it felt like the twist of a knife aimed straight at his heart.

God…I don't talk to You that much. But You were there with me when I begged for Your help—I could feel Your presence.

And now I'm asking for one more thing. Help me to do what's right for this child. Help me be the right kind of parent for him and to make the right choices. Because I know I can't do this alone.

He stood still for a moment, willing God to give him some sort of answer. But when none came, he carefully put Max back in his car seat and buckled him in.

And then he headed for Dallas.

EIGHTEEN

The days turned into weeks, then a month rolled past.

Erin methodically went about her business at the store, welcoming the new customers who had heard about the reopening, thanks to the news articles about Patrick and the time he'd spent hiding in the area.

But despite being busier now, the empty house next to the store echoed the empty place in her heart, and she hadn't been able to bring herself to move there. Not just yet.

"I'm done sweeping," Ollie said proudly.

"You always do a great job," she said with a smile. "And now that you're done, there's someone in the café who'd like to talk to both of us. Is that okay? You can have your coffee and rolls while we visit."

Ollie shook his head vehemently. "Bad lady," he whispered, glancing at the front door as if debating making a run for it. "*Bad*. I saw her."

"She's a social worker, Ollie."

"She tried to take me away." He gripped the broom handle tighter, his hands trembling. "Won't go. I *won't*."

"It's okay, I promise. We'll just talk." She took the broom from him and set it aside, then led him to a table in the café where Betsy Peters waited, her hands folded on top of several files. The silver-haired county social worker had met with Erin to discuss Ollie's situation several times during the past two weeks, and with luck, this meeting would go well.

He jerked to a halt when he saw her. "Not going," he said, his voice rising. "I won't!"

"We've tried convincing him to move to the county home for years, but he wouldn't go." Betsy smiled at Ollie. "But this is something different. Just have a seat, okay?"

He warily sat down, ignoring the coffee and caramel rolls that Erin set down in front of him. He gave her an accusing look.

"Ollie and I go way back," Betsy said, stirring sugar into her cup of tea. "The county has tried lots of options, but he never wanted to leave his childhood home. Right, Ollie?"

He bowed his head. "Mama's house."

"But you've lived there alone for how many years? At least ten or more. It's no longer safe."

He didn't look up.

"The house is actually in need of demolition. And with all the years of unpaid taxes, well…something just has to be done. Do you understand, Ollie?"

When he didn't answer, she gave Erin a quick glance.

"Your mama would want you to be safe and warm, Ollie," Erin said. "That house is terribly drafty, and it isn't insulated. And though the church ladies bring you food sometimes, they can't do it if the weather is bad. And then what?" She took a deep breath. "But we've got exciting news! There's a brand-new group home nearby that was finished just this year. It's about halfway between Barry's greenhouse and this store, so you could work at either place if you wanted to and you'd be really close."

He lumbered to his feet, his eyes filled with panic. *"No!"*

"You'll always have three good, hot meals a day—with your very own room and comfy living room with a TV." Betsy smiled warmly. "You could always go and come whenever you like. No one would make you stay inside. And you'd have people there for company. Friends. You wouldn't be alone. And you wouldn't ever go hungry."

"And there's even a nice little barn in back with gardening tools and lawn mowers." Erin rested a hand on his arm. "Your cats could come along, too, and stay out there."

His lower lip trembled.

"But the best part for me is that you'd be nice and close for visiting, Ollie. You could come here for coffee anytime." Erin said a swift, silent prayer. "Betsy says I can go see it today, if you'll come with us. Please? I'd love to do that. I hear the empty bedroom is the nicest one of all."

He stood for a long moment, his face a mask of granite. "It's close?"

"We can take a nice little shortcut through the timber and be there in fifteen minutes. Plus, I got to meet the other people who live there, and they were really nice. They'd just love to meet you, too. What do you say? All three of us can go for a visit."

She held her breath, praying he would agree.

When he finally looked up at her, his expression was sad and defeated. "Just visit?"

"Just visit. In fact, I think we'll get there in time for lunch, and I believe they're having baked chicken and mashed potatoes today. With cherry pie."

At that, his eyes widened. "Chicken? And *pie?*"

"If you like the place, then we can work on moving you there." Betsy shrugged. "If not, don't worry. We'll think about other options."

But at the awe in Ollie's eyes, Erin smiled with relief. If nothing else, the cherry pie and chicken were going to seal the deal.

And soon Ollie would have a far better life.

* * *

Erin wistfully watched a young couple walk out the front door of Millie's. Probably in their mid-twenties, they'd proudly showed off their new wedding rings and had bubbled on and on about their wedding on a beach near San Francisco.

It was wonderful to see people so happy, so filled with excitement over the future. Even Ollie was happier than she'd ever seen him. He'd moved into the group home two days after his tour, and twice now he'd shown up at Millie's with a different new friend in tow.

If only...

But Jack had been in an obvious hurry to leave, and she hadn't heard from him since. No matter what she'd felt for him, it had clearly been one-sided. Though sometimes, during the long evenings, she sat with Charlie on the porch swing and relived those last days when Jack and Max were still here.

If she'd been more open, would things have ended any differently? Had she really ever seen that gleam of interest in his eyes—or had it been only her imagination?

At the sound of a car door slamming, she turned and dredged up a friendly smile, shelving her melancholy thoughts.

A child's footsteps raced across the porch, and the front door burst open.

And there was Max, smiling from ear to ear, his eyes sparkling and cheeks flushed. "Surprise!"

Stunned, she stared at him, unsure for a heartbeat whether he was real or an apparition.

But Charlie heard him, too. The dog scrambled to his feet and bounded across the store, tongue lolling and tail wagging furiously.

"Charlie!" Max wrapped his arms around the dog's neck and buried his face in the fur. "I missed you, Charlie." A heartbeat later he ran to Erin, and when she lifted him high, he wrapped his arms around her neck. "We *had* to come back. We drove and drove and *drove*."

She gave him a kiss on the cheek. "I'm so glad, Max—I missed you both so much. And Charlie did, too. Are you hungry?"

He nodded vigorously. "You are the best cooker ever. But don't tell Uncle Jack."

Without looking up, she sensed the moment Jack appeared in the doorway. She lifted her gaze slowly, taking him in. Tall, broad-shouldered, with that dark, wavy hair and those deep dimples bracketing his mouth, he looked like someone who could ride to her rescue on a black stallion, sweep her up behind him and thunder off into the sunset.

"We had to come back," he said simply, striding over to stand in front of her. He looked down at her, his eyes twinkling. "Max made sure I knew it was a big mistake for us to leave, but I knew it, too."

"A mistake?" she asked faintly. She gave Max an extra hug and then put him down. "What kind of mistake?"

"Let's go outside for a few minutes." She followed him to the porch swing, with Max and Charlie tagging along behind them.

As soon as she sat next to Jack on the swing, Charlie jumped up to join them, and Max squeezed in at her other side.

"I've been wanting to ask you something," he continued. "It's probably the wrong place, and it's definitely the wrong time. But I just can't wait any longer."

Her heart started to flutter.

"We haven't known each other for very long…yet I feel like I've known you forever." His deep, gentle voice was like a caress. "I know you've made a commitment to your grandfather, and that you need to stay here. But if I move back to Texas permanently, we might lose something that's too precious to risk."

A tentative ray of hope began to flicker in her chest when he cupped her cheek with his hand, then brushed a kiss over her lips.

"I just want to know if there's any chance…for us."

The tender emotion in his eyes nearly took her breath away. "I've never wanted anything more."

With a fifty-pound mass of fur lying across them on the swing, it was nearly impossible to move, but she ached to turn into Jack's arms.

"Charlie, you really need to go," she murmured. *"Now."*

Maybe the dog understood what this moment meant, because he eased out of the swing and moved to a corner of the porch without protest and, grinning, Max hopped down to follow him.

With Charlie out of the way, she curved her arms around Jack's neck and drew him into a kiss that made her feel breathless and giddy.

And when he kissed her back, she felt as if she'd joined the stars above.

* * * * *

Be sure to look for Roxanne Rustand's next book in the BIG SKY SECRETS *miniseries, available in February 2010, wherever Steeple Hill books are sold!*

Dear Reader,

Welcome to the beautiful Montana Rockies and the start of my BIG SKY SECRETS trilogy. The other two books will be out in February 2010 and June 2010. I hope you will mark your calendar and join me for the ongoing stories of these three young women. A terrible tragedy may have marked their high-school years, but each of them has grown up to be a strong, resourceful woman ready to face the challenges and dangers ahead in their own lives.

In *Final Exposure,* Erin remembers a Bible passage that means a lot to me, too. *Don't worry about anything; instead, pray about everything. Tell God what you need, and thank Him for all He has done. If you do this, you will experience God's peace, which is far more wonderful than the human mind can understand. His peace will guard your hearts and minds as you live in Jesus Christ.* Philippians 4:6, 7

What wonderful reassurance this is! This passage has helped me through some difficult times, bringing me peace and comfort. If you are facing tough times, I hope you will turn to the Lord, too, and speak to Him in prayer. He will never let you down.

If you'd like to contact me, you can do so through www.roxannerustand.com. I also have a blog at:

www.shoutlife.com/roxannerustand.
And if you'd like to visit a host of authors who write
for Love Inspired Suspense, you can find us at:
 http://ladiesofsuspense.blogspot.com.

Wishing you abundant blessings and peace,

Roxanne

DISCUSSION QUESTIONS

1. Erin's life has been marked forever by the murder of her cousin in high school. Were there any tragedies or hardships in your own youth that still affect you as an adult?

2. Greed drove Ted to embezzle from his vulnerable, elderly clients. What does the Bible say about forgiveness? Do you think Ted could ever be forgiven for his crimes? What about the crimes Patrick committed?

3. Ollie is a low-functioning adult, but pride, fear and attachment to his late parents' home have kept him from using government services that are available to him. What types of services are available in your area for folks in need? What kinds of volunteer opportunities are there? Is there anything you could do to help—maybe as a family or with a group from your church?

4. Max is devastated by the loss of his parents. Do children grieve differently than adults? Look up John 3:16. What reassurance does this verse offer to all of us? How would you explain this verse to a young child?

5. Both Erin and Jack pray for help at different times during the story. How are their prayers answered? Are they answered right away? God answers our prayers, but in his own perfect time, and sometimes in ways we may never have thought of in advance. Discuss how your own prayers have been answered.

6. Jack is wary of commitment after his fiancée ends their engagement while he is struggling with Ted's embezzlement, the tarnished reputation of his company and becoming a single parent. Read 1 Corinthians 13. What are your feelings about love and commitment, through good times and bad?

7. How did God answer Erin's prayers for help when her life was in danger at the end of the book?

8. Jack's sister and brother-in-law, both strong Christians, died in a car accident. At the beginning of the story, Jack is angry at God for not saving them. Why do terrible things sometimes happen to good people? What does the Bible say about this?

10. Initially Jack only wants to go to church so that Max can continue the traditions of his late par-

ents. How effective will this be? Discuss the nurturing of faith in young children.

11. Jack has gladly taken on the job of parenting his orphaned nephew, and is struggling to do the best job he can. Have you ever shouldered extra responsibilities to help a family member in need? What is the best piece of parenting advice that you could give Jack?

Private investigator Wade Sutton plans to hightail
it out of Dry Creek long before December 25.
The town holds too many unmerry memories.
Until he's asked to watch over a woman in danger,
a woman whose faith changes him forever.

Turn the page for a sneak preview of
SILENT NIGHT IN DRY CREEK
by Janet Tronstad.
Available in October 2009
from Love Inspired®

Wade wished he had never come back to Dry Creek. Or, since he had come back, he wished people hadn't been so kind to him. Barbara making that cake for him was putting him off his game. And then Jasmine—usually he didn't have any trouble taking a tough line with a suspect. But then, he'd never been tempted to kiss a suspect before.

He watched Jasmine's back as she walked to the table. She was ramrod straight and angry with him. He knew he'd come on too strong, but it was either that or forgetting everything he knew about law enforcement and refusing to believe she could be responsible for anything.

As a lawman he had to consider all the possibilities, and it was hard to forget that Lonnie had been her partner. She could have sent him a coded message that in some way had helped him escape from prison, or at least given him an incentive to risk everything to get outside.

He wished he knew how to look into the heart of a person so he would know what Jasmine was thinking. Was she as innocent as she looked, or as guilty as she had been the first time she was convicted of a crime? He knew better than most how many ex-cons fell back into theft. He was often the one who took them in the second time around and listened to their sorry excuses.

"I gave you the biggest piece of cake," Barbara said as he sat down at his place at the table.

"Thank you." Wade smiled. It was the cake of his childhood fantasies, and he was going to have to force himself to eat it. All he wanted to do was take Jasmine home and then park his car at the end of the lane to her father's place. Why did she have to be tied up with Lonnie? Why couldn't she be a nice, ordinary woman like Barbara here? Carl never had to worry about arresting *her.*

Wade felt the smoothness of the cake on his tongue and the sweet tang of the raspberry filling. He smiled up at Barbara and thanked her again for the cake. The two kids at the table were smacking their lips and demanding more, just as Wade would be doing if he wasn't so troubled.

Then he looked down the table and saw his dear friend Edith. She wouldn't be happy about him keeping an eye on anyone. It was clear the older woman was very fond of Jasmine. That, of course, was the problem with being a lawman and trying to have friends. He liked things black and white with no shades of gray. He didn't want to have feelings for the suspect.

By doing his job, he was going to upset Jasmine and everyone else in Dry Creek. For the first time since he'd driven into town, he missed the barren feel of his apartment in Idaho Falls. He knew who he was there.

It didn't take long for Wade to leave the Walls's house, with Jasmine walking in front of him. The night was cold. Jasmine wrapped her arms around her body to keep warm and hurried to his car. He was still nursing that leg of his, so he went more slowly than she did. He made it in good time, though, and as he opened the car door for her, she nodded her thanks and slid into the passenger seat.

The first thing Wade did after he got into the car was to move the dial up on the heater. Snowflakes were just starting to fall, but they were scattered enough that he could clear them away with his windshield wipers.

He silently turned his car around and started down the sheriff's lane. The car lights shone on the falling snow, making the flakes look like pinpricks in the darkness.

"You don't think Lonnie would do something to my father, do you?" Jasmine asked. She looked up at him with eyes full of worry. "Lonnie's not very stable. I wouldn't want anyone around here to be hurt by him."

Wade shrugged. "With all you'd inherit if Elmer were out of the picture—"

Jasmine gasped. "I don't care about the money."

"Lonnie might."

That turned her quiet. He didn't want her to worry, though.

"He won't even have the chance to get close to anyone," Wade assured her. "We'll have the feds all over the place by tomorrow. Lonnie has a better chance of breaking in to Fort Knox than he has of sneaking into Dry Creek."

Wade hoped he wasn't lying. He had no idea what the feds would do. And they might have some completely different theories as to why Lonnie had broken out of prison. It might have nothing at all to do with Jasmine or anyone in Dry Creek.

"You'll be safe," Wade said as he opened his door.

He walked around to the passenger door and opened it. Wade stood by the open car door and watched as Jasmine pulled her coat closer to her body. She wasn't making any move to walk toward the house and he wasn't making any move to let her. Finally Wade reached out and touched her cheek. It was soft and a little damp. She must have been crying when she'd been huddled against the door on the drive out here.

"It'll be okay," he whispered to her as he brought his hand down.

"I'm fine," she said.

He nodded with a slight smile. "I know."

Wade had never kissed a suspect, but he would have done it now if he hadn't thought it would make Jasmine cry even more. She was barely hanging on, and he needed to leave her with her dignity.

"I'll be parked at the end of Elmer's lane if you need me," Wade said as he stepped back from the door. Snow was falling in earnest now, but in his trunk he had a heavy sleeping bag that he used on stakeouts like this. "I'll come to the door in the morning, before I go over to my grandfather's."

"You can't sleep outside all night. It's freezing out here. I'll leave the kitchen door unlocked in case you need to come inside."

"Don't leave anything unlocked. I'll duck into the barn if I need to."

Jasmine nodded.

Wade watched her walk to the kitchen door and go inside the house. Only then did he head back to the driver's door. He wondered if he'd get any sleep tonight. He was losing his edge. The next thing he knew, he was going to be offering pillows to everyone he arrested and wishing them sweet dreams. When had he turned into a soft touch?

He waited for the light to go out in the kitchen before he started his drive down the lane. He already felt lonely.

* * * * *

Will Jasmine give Wade reason to
call Dry Creek home again?
Find out in
SILENT NIGHT IN DRY CREEK
by Janet Tronstad.
Available in October 2009
from Love Inspired®

For private investigator
Wade Sutton, Dry Creek
holds too many memories—
and none of them fond.
Yet he can't say no when
the sheriff asks him to
watch over a woman
who might be in danger.
Getting to know lovely
Jasmine Hunter just might
give Wade a good reason
to call Dry Creek home
once more....

Look for
Silent Night in Dry Creek
by
Janet Tronstad

*Available October
wherever books are sold.*

Steeple
Hill®

LI87553

www.SteepleHill.com

Love Inspired®

HEARTWARMING INSPIRATIONAL ROMANCE

Get more of the heartwarming inspirational romance stories that you love and cherish, beginning in July with SIX NEW titles, available every month from the Love Inspired® line.

Also look for our other
Love Inspired® genres, including:

Love Inspired® Suspense:
Enjoy four contemporary tales of intrigue and romance every month.

Love Inspired® Historical:
Travel to a different time with two powerful and engaging stories of romance, adventure and faith every month.

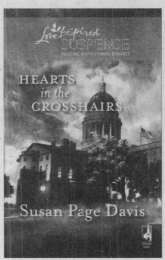

REQUEST YOUR FREE BOOKS!

2 FREE RIVETING INSPIRATIONAL NOVELS
PLUS 2 FREE MYSTERY GIFTS

Love Inspired.
SUSPENSE

YES! Please send me 2 FREE Love Inspired® Suspense novels and my 2 FREE mystery gifts (gifts are worth about $10). After receiving them, if I don't wish to receive any more books, I can return the shipping statement marked "cancel". If I don't cancel, I will receive 4 brand-new novels every month and be billed just $4.24 per book in the U.S. or $4.74 per book in Canada. That's a savings of over 20% off the cover price. It's quite a bargain! Shipping and handling is just 50¢ per book.* I understand that accepting the 2 free books and gifts places me under no obligation to buy anything. I can always return a shipment and cancel at any time. Even if I never buy another book, the two free books and gifts are mine to keep forever.

123 IDN EYM2 323 IDN EYNE

Name	(PLEASE PRINT)

Address	Apt. #

City	State/Prov.	Zip/Postal Code

Signature (if under 18, a parent or guardian must sign)

Mail to Steeple Hill Reader Service:

IN U.S.A.: P.O. Box 1867, Buffalo, NY 14240-1867
IN CANADA: P.O. Box 609, Fort Erie, Ontario L2A 5X3

Not valid to current subscribers of Love Inspired Suspense books.

Want to try two free books from another series?
Call 1-800-873-8635 or visit www.morefreebooks.com

* Terms and prices subject to change without notice. Prices do not include applicable taxes. Sales tax applicable in N.Y. Canadian residents will be charged applicable provincial taxes and GST. Offer not valid in Quebec. This offer is limited to one order per household. All orders subject to approval. Credit or debit balances in a customer's account(s) may be offset by any other outstanding balance owed by or to the customer. Please allow 4 to 6 weeks for delivery. Offer available while quantities last.

Your Privacy: Steeple Hill Books is committed to protecting your privacy. Our Privacy Policy is available online at www.SteepleHill.com or upon request from the Reader Service. From time to time we make our lists of customers available to reputable third parties who may have a product or service of interest to you. If you would prefer we not share your name and address, please check here. ☐

LISUS09

Love Inspired
HISTORICAL

INSPIRATIONAL HISTORICAL ROMANCE

After years of caring for others, Nola Burns is ready to live her own dream of running a Nantucket tearoom. And it will take more than charm for dashing entrepreneur Harrison Starbuck to buy her out. All Harry offers is a business proposition. So why should it bother him when Nola starts receiving threatening notes? As the threats escalate, he realizes he wants to keep her safe…forever.

Look for

An Unexpected Suitor
by
ANNA SCHMIDT

Available October wherever books are sold.

www.SteepleHill.com

Love Inspired®
SUSPENSE

TITLES AVAILABLE NEXT MONTH

Available October 13, 2009

HEARTS IN THE CROSSHAIRS by Susan Page Davis

She came to be inaugurated—and left dodging bullets.
Dave Hutchins of Maine's Executive Protection Unit doesn't
know who wants to kill governor Jillian Goff. Still, he won't
let her get hurt on his watch, not even when he finds his
own heart getting caught in the crosshairs.

GUARDED SECRETS by Leann Harris

"If I die, it won't be an accident." Lilly Burkstrom can't
forget her ex-husband's words...especially after his
"accidental" death. As her fear builds, the only person this
single mother can trust is Detective Jonathan Littledeer.
Can he keep Lilly safe?

TRIAL BY FIRE by Cara Putman

Her mother's house was first. Then her brother's. County
prosecutor Tricia Jamison is sure she's next on the arsonist's
list. But who is after her family? And why does every fire
throw her in the path of Noah Brust, the firefighter who
can't forgive or forget their shared past?

DÉJÀ VU by Jenness Walker

Cole Leighton can barely believe it when a woman on his
bus is abducted—in an *exact* reflection of a scene from the
bestseller he's reading. Someone's bringing the book to life...
and Kenzie Jacobs is trapped in the grisly story. Now the
killer is writing his own ending, and none of the twists and
turns lead to happily ever after.